John Christopher

The City of Gold and Lead

Aladdin Paperbacks

First Aladdin Paperbacks edition 1970
Second Aladdin Paperbacks edition 1988
Revised cover edition, 1999

Aladdin Paperbacks
An imprint of Simon & Schuster Children's Publishing Division
1230 Avenue of the Americas
New York, NY 10020

Printed and bound in the United States of America
OPM 33 32 31 30 29 28 27 26 25

Library of Congress Cataloging-in-Publication Data
Christopher, John
The city of gold and lead.
The 2nd vol. of the author's trilogy entitled The Tripods trilogy; the 1st
of which is The White Mountains, and the 3rd, The pool of fire.
Summary: Three boys set out on a secret mission to penetrate
the City of the Tripods and learn more about these
strange beings that rule the earth.
[1. Science fiction] I. Title. II. Title: Tripods trilogy.
PZ7.C457Ci   1988   [Fic]   88-16118
ISBN 0-02-042701-8

Contents

1

Three Are Chosen

One day Julius called a conference of the instructors, and all training was canceled. The three of us—Henry, Beanpole, and I—decided to use the free time to explore the upper reaches of the tunnel. So we got picnic rations from the kitchen and half a dozen big, slow-burning tallow candles, and set off up the long winding slope from the caves in which we lived.

At first we chattered as we went, hearing our voices echo from the confining walls of rock, but as our progress became more slogging and arduous we talked less, conserving our strength. The ancients had made the tunnel to house a Shmand-Fair—a railway as it had once been called in my own language—and the metal tracks went up and up, interminably it seemed. The candles gave only a small and flickering light, but a sure one; there was no wind, not even a breeze, that might blow them out. We were climbing a mountain, but from the inside.

I puzzled over this, as I had done before. It was one of countless riddles left by our forefathers, but more baffling than most and, of course, nearer at hand. Even with the wonderful machines we knew they had possessed, it must have taken a tremendous time—years—to hew such a channel through the heart of this stony giant. For what purpose? A railway leading to a mountain top, perpetually covered with snow and ice? It made no sense that I could see.

They had been a strange and marvelous people. I had seen the ruins of one of the great-cities in which they lived . . . with broad avenues that ran for miles, crumbling buildings still soaring up against the sky, huge shops into which all the houses of my native village could have been packed, with room left over. They had moved in ease and splendor about the earth, splendor beyond measuring, almost beyond understanding. And despite all this, the Tripods had conquered and enslaved them. How had it happened? We did not know. We only knew that, except for the handful of us who lived here in the White Mountains, men did the Tripods' bidding, and did it gladly.

The way in which they kept their domination, on the other hand, was plain enough. It was done through the Caps, meshes of silvery metal, fitting closely round the skull and woven into the very flesh of their wearers. Capping took place in one's fourteenth year, marking the change from child to adult. A Tripod took you away, and a Tripod brought you back. Those who returned, apart from the few who cracked under the ordeal and became Vagrants and thereafter wandered aimlessly from place to place, had had their minds changed and were free no longer.

We went on, higher and higher, through the tunnel. Occasionally we rested, easing the ache in our legs, sometimes at places where there were openings through which one could see out of the mountain side to a vista of more mountains and cold, deserted snowfields lying in their shadow. If we had realized how long and arduous the journey would be, I doubt if we should have embarked on it, but having come so far we pressed on. We found small things—a button, a carton that said CAMELS and had a picture of a beast like a humpbacked horse on it, and a scrap of newspaper, printed in the German language which we were learning, that spoke of incomprehensible things. All these were more than a hundred years old, we knew, relics from the world before the Tripods.

At last we reached the cavern where the railway ended. There were stone steps, leading to a room in what seemed like a palace. Higher still, in a vast wooden hall, we stared through gigantic windows at a scene of wonder. There were peaks all round, guarding a valley through which a river ran far into the distance. But the peaks glistened white, dazzling in sunlight that hurt the eyes, and the river was a river of ice that yet seemed to flow. Had a king perhaps lived here—a king who ruled the world, and chose to live on the world's roof?

But would the hall of a king's palace be filled with small tables, and have kitchens adjoining it? We explored farther, and found a sign: HOTEL JUNGFAUJOCH. I knew what a hotel was: a large inn that accommodated travelers. But here, on a mountain top? The idea was as mysterious as the idea of a royal palace, and more stupendous. It had not been a king and his courtiers who had walked through these echoing rooms and looked at the river of ice among the eternal snows; but ordinary men and women. A strange and marvelous people, indeed. In those days, I thought, they were all kings and queens.

I gazed out. Nothing changed there, nor had changed in a century. For me, so much had changed.

Six months earlier I had been an ordinary schoolboy living, as I had always done, in the village of Wherton, a day's journey by packhorse from Winchester. My cousin Jack, the companion of my childhood, had already been Capped; and I was to be Capped the next year, along with Henry, another cousin, but an old enemy rather than an old friend. After that I would be a man, working as a man, in due course taking over my father's mill, living in Wherton and at last dying there, to be buried in the churchyard beside the square-towered church. It was a pattern of life that everyone took for granted.

Then, one day, Ozymandias came to the village, a Vagrant seemingly, a big, red-haired, red-bearded man, who sang songs and spoke lines of poetry, and mixed sense and nonsense when he talked. He sounded me out, and finally revealed himself and his purpose. He was not a Vagrant, but merely posing as such so that he could travel without hindrance or suspicion. The

Cap he wore was a false one. He told me the truth about the Tripods, and told me also of the handful of free un-Capped men who lived far to the south. He asked me if I would be willing to make a difficult and dangerous journey to join them.

So, with the map and compass he had given me, I left my village. Henry surprised me while I was making my escape, and I was forced to take him with me. We crossed the sea together, and in the land called France found a third—Jean-Paul, whom we named Beanpole because he was so tall and thin. Together, we went south. It was as difficult and dangerous as Ozymandias had promised. Near the end we fought a battle with a Tripod, and with the help of a weapon of the ancients that we found in the ruins of one of the great-cities, destroyed it. And thus came to the White Mountains.

There were eleven of us in the training cadre being prepared for the first move in the counter-attack against our enemies. It was a hard schooling, in body and mind alike, but we knew a little of the task before us, and how heavy the odds against success were. The discipline and hardship we had to endure might not shorten those odds by much, but every bit counted.

For we—or some of us—were to conduct a reconnaissance. We knew almost nothing of the Tripods, not even whether they were intelligent machines or vehicles for other creatures. We had to know more before we could hope to fight them successfully and there was only one way to get that knowledge. Some of us, one at least, must penetrate into the City of the Tripods, study them, and bring back information.

The plan was this: the City lay to the north, in the country of the Germans. Each year some of the newly Capped were brought there to serve the Tripods. They were chosen in different ways. I had witnessed one such way at the Château de la Tour Rouge, when Eloise, the daughter of the Comte, had been made Queen of the Tournament. I had been horrified to learn that at the end of her brief reign she would be taken to be a slave of the enemy, and go gladly, thinking it an honor.

Among the Germans, it seemed, there were Games each summer, to which young men came from all over the land. The winners were feasted and made much of, after which they, too, went to serve in the City. At the next Games, it was hoped, one of us might win, and gain admission. What would happen after that was unknown. Anyone who succeeded would have to rely on his wits, both in spying on the Tripods and in passing on what he had learned. The last part

was likely to be the hardest. Because although
scores, perhaps hundreds, went yearly into the
City, not one had ever been known to come out.

One day the snow was melting at the foot of
the tunnel where we exercised, and a week later
it lay only in isolated patches, and there was the
green of grass, dotted with purple crocuses. The
sky was blue, and sunlight flamed from the
white peaks all round, burning our skins
through the thin, pure air. During a break we
lay on the grass and looked down. Figures
moved cautiously half a mile below, visible to
us but taking cover from those who might look
up from the valley. This was the first raiding
party of the season on its way to plunder the fat
lands of the Capped.

I sat with Henry and Beanpole, a little apart
from the rest. The lives of all those who lived in
the mountain were closely knit, but this strand
was a more tightly woven one. In the things we
had endured, jealousies and enmities had worn
away and been replaced by true comradeship.
The boys in the cadre were our friends, but the
bond between us three was special.

Beanpole said gloomily, "I failed at one meter
seventy today." He spoke in German. We had
learned the language but needed to practice it.

I said, "One goes off form. You'll improve
again."

"I'm getting worse every day."

Henry said, "Rodrigo's gone off. I beat him comfortably."

"It's all right for you."

Henry had been chosen as a long-distance runner, and Rodrigo was his chief rival. Beanpole was training for long and high jumping. I was one of two boxers. There were four sports in all—the other was sprint running—and they had been arranged to produce a maximum of competitiveness. Henry had done well in his event from the start. I myself was fairly confident, at any rate as far as my opponent here was concerned. This was Tonio, a dark-skinned boy from the south, taller than I and with a longer reach, but not as quick. Beanpole, though, had grown increasingly pessimistic about his chances.

Henry reassured him, telling him he had heard the instructors saying he was coming on well. I wondered if it were true or said for encouragement: the former, I hoped.

I said, "I asked Johann if it had been decided yet how many were to go."

Johann, one of the instructors, was squat and powerful, yellow-haired, with the look of a bad-tempered bull but amiable at heart.

Henry asked, "What did he say?"

"He wasn't sure, but he thought four—the best from each group."

"So it could be us three, plus an extra," Henry said.

Beanpole shook his head. "I'll never do it."

"You will."

I said, "And the fourth?"

"It might be Fritz."

He did seem to be the best of the sprint runners, as far as we could tell. He was German, and came from a place on the edge of a forest to the northeast. His chief rival was a French boy, Etienne, whom I preferred. Etienne was cheerful and talkative; Fritz, tall, heavy, taciturn.

I said, "As long as we all get through."

"You two will," Beanpole said.

Henry leaped to his feet. "There's the whistle. Come on, Beanpole. Time to get back to work."

The seniors had their own tasks. Some were our instructors; others formed the raiding parties to keep us supplied with food. There were still others who studied the few books that had survived from olden days and tried to relearn the skills and mysteries of our ancestors. Beanpole, whenever he had a chance, would be with them, listening to their talk and even putting up suggestions of his own. Not long after we met he had spoken—wildly, I thought—about using a sort of gigantic kettle to push carriages without the need for horses. Something like this had been discovered, or rediscovered, here, though it would not yet work properly. And there were plans for more remarkable things: making light and heat through something that had been called electricity was one.

And at the head of all the groups there was one man, whose hands held all the threads, whose decisions were unquestioned. This was Julius.

He was close to sixty years old, a small man, and a cripple. When he was a boy he had fallen into an ice crevasse and broken his thigh. It had been set badly and he walked with a limp. In those days things had been very different in the White Mountains. Those who lived there had no purpose but survival, and their numbers were dwindling. It was Julius who thought of winning recruits from the world outside, from those not yet Capped, and who believed—and made others believe—that someday men would fight back against the Tripods and destroy them.

It was Julius, too, who had worked out the enterprise for which we were being trained. And it was Julius who would make the final decision on which of us were chosen.

He came out one day to watch us. He was white-haired and red-cheeked, like most of those who had lived all their lives in this sharp, clear air, and he leaned on a stick. I saw him, and concentrated hard on the bout in which I was engaged. Tonio feinted with his left and followed up with a right cross. I made him miss, hammered a sharp right to his ribs, and, when he came in again, landed a left to the jaw, which sent him sprawling.

Julius beckoned, and I ran to where he stood. He said, "You are improving, Will."

"Thank you, sir."

"I suppose you are getting impatient to know which of you will be going to the Games."

I nodded. "A little, sir."

He studied me. "When the Tripod had you in its grasp—do you remember how you felt? Were you afraid?"

I remembered. I said, "Yes, sir."

"And the thought of being in their hands, in their City—does that frighten you?" I hesitated, and he went on. "There are two sides to the choice, you know. We old ones may be able to judge your quickness and skill of mind and body, but we cannot read your hearts."

"Yes," I admitted, "it frightens me."

"You do not have to go. You can be useful here." His pale blue eyes looked into mine. "No one need know if you prefer to stay."

I said, "I want to go. I can bear the thought of being in their hands more easily than the thought of being left behind."

"Good." He smiled. "And you, after all, have killed a Tripod—something that I doubt any other human being can claim. It is an asset to have that knowledge that they are not all-powerful."

"Do you mean, sir . . . ?"

"I mean what I said. There are other considerations. You must go on working hard, and preparing, in case you are chosen."

Later I saw him talking to Henry. I thought it was probably much the same conversation as mine had been. I did not ask him, though, and he did not volunteer anything about it.

During the winter our diet, although adequate, had been very dull, the staple item dried and salted meat that, whatever was done with it, remained stodgy and unappetizing. In the middle of April, though, a raiding party brought back half a dozen black-and-white cows, and Julius decreed that one should be killed and roasted. After the feast, he spoke to us. When he had been talking a few minutes, I realized, the excitement almost suffocating me, that this, almost certainly, was the moment for announcing the names of those who were to make the attempt at reconnoitering the City of the Tripods.

He had a quiet voice, and I was with the other boys at the far end of the cave, but his words were clear. Everyone was listening attentively and in silence. I glanced at Henry, on my right. In the flickering light, I thought he looked very confident. My own confidence was ebbing rapidly. It would be bitter if he went and I were left.

First, Julius talked about the plan in general. For months those in the training cadre had been training for their task. They would have some advantage over competitors from the lower lands, because it was known that men in higher altitudes developed stronger lungs and muscles than those who lived in the thicker air. But it had to be remembered that there would be hundreds of competitors drawn from the best athletes all over the country. It might be that, for all their preparation, not one of our small band would wear a champion's belt. In that case, they must find their way back to the White Mountains. We would try again, next year. Patience was as necessary as determination.

Contestants in the Games must be Capped, of course. That presented no great difficulty. We had Caps, taken from those killed in forays into the valleys, which could be molded to fit the skulls of the ones chosen. They would look like true Caps, but they would not control the mind.

Now to the details: the City of the Tripods lay hundreds of miles to the north. There was a great river that covered most of that distance. Barges plied up and down it in trade, and one of these was in the hands of our men. It would sail to a spot within easy reach of the place where the Games were held.

Julius paused before going on.

It had been decided that three should be selected from the training cadre. Many things had to be taken into account: individual skill and strength, the likely level of competition in the event, the temperament of the person, and his probable usefulness once he had penetrated the Tripods' stronghold. It had not been easy, but the choices had been made. Raising his voice slightly, he called, "Stand up, Will Parker."

For all my hopes, the shock of hearing my own name unnerved me. My legs trembled as I got to my feet.

Julius said, "You have shown ability as a boxer, Will, and you have the advantage of being small and light in weight. Your training has been with Tonio, who would be in a heavier class at the Games, and this should help you.

"The doubt we had was about you yourself. You are impatient, often thoughtless, likely to rush into things without giving careful enough consideration to what may happen next. From that point of view, Tonio would have been better. But he is less likely to succeed at the Games, which is our first concern. A heavy responsibility may rest on you. Can we rely on you to do your utmost to guard against your own recklessness?"

I promised, "Yes, sir."

"Sit down, then, Will. Stand up, Jean-Paul Deliet."

I think I felt gladder about Beanpole than when my own name was called, perhaps because I was less confused and had been less optimistic. I had picked up his own gloom about his chances. So there would be three—the three of us who had journeyed together before, who had fought the Tripod on the hillside.

Julius said, "There were difficulties in your case, too, Jean-Paul. You are the best of our jumpers, but it is not sure that you are up to the standard that will be necessary to win at the Games. And there is the question of your eyesight. The contraption of lenses you invented— or rediscovered, because they were common among the ancients—is something that passed as an eccentricity in a boy, but the Capped do not have such eccentricities. Not being allowed to wear the lenses, you must blunder through a world in which you will see less clearly than your fellows. If you get inside the City, you will not perceive things with the clarity that Will, for instance, would.

"But what you see, you may understand better. Your intelligence is an asset that outweighs the weakness of your eyes. You could be the most useful in bringing back to us what we have to know. Do you accept the task?"

Beanpole said, "Yes, sir."

"And so we come to the third choice, which was the easiest." I saw Henry looking pleased with himself, and was childish enough to feel a little resentment. "He is the most likely to succeed in his event, and the best equipped for what may follow.

"Fritz Eger—do you accept?"

I tried to speak to Henry, but he made it plain that he wanted to be left alone. I saw him again later on, but he was morose and uncommunicative. Then, the following morning, I happened to go to the lookout gallery, and found him there.

It was the lowest of the places where openings in the mountain side gave a view of the outside world. One looked out and down to a rich green valley, thousands of feet below, in which there were roads like black thread, tiny houses, pinpoint cattle in miniature meadows. Henry was leaning against the low wall of rock and turned as I approached. I said awkwardly, "If you want me to go . . ."

"No." He shrugged. "It doesn't matter."

"I'm . . . very sorry."

He managed a grin. "Not as sorry as I am."

"If we went to see Julius . . . I don't see why there shouldn't be four instead of three."

"I've already seen him."

"And there's no hope?"

"None. I'm the best of my lot, but they don't think I stand much chance in the Games. Perhaps next year, if I keep at it."

"I don't see why you shouldn't *try* this year."

"I said that, too. He says even three is really too large a party to send out. So much more chance of being spotted, and more difficult with the barge."

One did not argue with Julius. I said, "Well, you will have a chance next year."

"If there is a next year."

There would only be a second expedition if this one failed. I thought of what failure could mean, to me personally. The diminutive valley of fields and houses and ribboned rivers, on which I had so often looked with longing, was as sunny as before, but suddenly less attractive. I was staring at it from a dark hole, but one in which I had come to feel safe.

Yet even in the brush of fear, I felt sorry for Henry. I could have been the one left behind. I did not think I would have borne it as well, if so.

2

Prisoner
in the Pit

We set out in late afternoon, made our way secretly through the nearer valleys during dusk, and traveled on by moonlight. We did not rest until the sun was high, and by then we were halfway along the shore of the westerly of the twin lakes that lay below our stronghold. We hid ourselves on the hillside; behind and far above us was the glistening white peak from which we had started our journey. We were tired. We ate, and then slept, exhausted, through the long hot day.

It was a hundred miles to the point on the river at which we were to join the *Erlkönig*. We had a guide—one of the men who knew the country from raiding parties—who would go with us as far as the barge. We went mostly by night, resting during the daylight hours.

This was some weeks after the feast, and Julius's announcement. During that time we had been given further instruction and preparation, starting with having our hair cropped short and the false Cap molded to fit close to our skulls. It had been strange and desperately uncomfortable at first, but gradually I had grown used to this hard helmet of metal. My hair was already growing through and around the mesh, and we were assured that before the Games began we should look no different from other boys who had been Capped, in the first weeks of summer, as they were here. At night we wore bonnets of wool, because otherwise the cold would strike through the metal, painfully waking us.

Henry had not been among those who watched us leave the tunnel. I understood that. I would not have wanted to be there if our situations had been reversed. My impulse was to resent Fritz, who had taken his place, but I remembered what Julius had said about needing to curb my rashness. I remembered also that I had resented what I thought was the greater friendship between Beanpole and Henry on our journey south, and how I had allowed it to influence me during our stay at the Château de la Tour Rouge.

I was determined not to let anything of that kind happen now, and with this in mind made a special effort to overcome my animosity and be nice to Fritz. But there was a poor response to my overtures; he remained taciturn and withdrawn. I was prepared to resent that, in turn and with more justification, as I saw it. But I succeeded in bottling up my annoyance. It was a great help that Beanpole was with us. He and I did most of the talking, when we were in circumstances where talking did not involve risk. Our guide, Primo, a dark, burly man, looking clumsy but in fact wonderfully sure-footed, said little beyond what was necessary in warning and instruction.

A week had been allowed for us to reach the barge, but we covered the distance in four days. We followed a high ridge, skirting the ruins of one of the great-cities. These encompassed a bend in the river, which was to be our thoroughfare. The river came from the east, with the early morning sun glinting along its length, but here turned and flowed northward. The higher stretch was empty, as was the part that ran between the sullen humps that had once been tow-

ering buildings, but above that there was traffic
—two barges nosing downriver, perhaps a dozen
tied up by the bank at the wharves of a small
town.

Primo pointed down. "One of those will be the
Erlkönig. You can find your way down there on
your own?"

We assured him that we could.

"Then I'll be getting back." He nodded briefly.
"Good luck to you."

The *Erlkönig* was one of the smaller barges,
some fifty feet in length. There was nothing
special about her; she was just a long, low structure rising a few feet above the surface of the
water, with a partly covered wheelhouse aft,
giving the steersman some protection against the
elements. She had a crew of two, both false-
Capped. The senior of them was called Ulf, a
squat, barrel-chested man in his forties, with a
brusque manner and a habit of punctuating his
speech by spitting. I did not like him, the more
so after he made a disparaging remark about my
slightness of build. His companion, Moritz, was
about ten years younger and, I thought, ten
times pleasanter. He had fair hair, a thin face,
and a warm and ready smile. But there could
be no doubt as to which of them was master:
Moritz deferred to Ulf automatically. And it was

Ulf, spitting and grunting at regular intervals, who gave us our instructions for the voyage.

"We're a two-man barge," he told us. "An extra boy is fair enough—you start 'prentices that way. But any more would draw notice, and I'm not having it. So you'll take it in turns to work on deck—and when I say work, boy, I mean it —and the other two will lie below decks and won't come up even if she's foundering. You've been told the need for discipline, I take it, so I don't need to go into that. All I want to say is this: I shall give short shrift to anyone who causes trouble, for whatever reason.

"I know the job you've got to do, and I hope you're up to it. But if you can't behave sensibly and obey orders on this trip, you're not likely to be any good later on. So I won't think twice about dropping somebody off who's out of line. And since I wouldn't want him to float into the wrong harbor and start people asking questions, I've got a weight of iron to tie his legs to before I do drop him off."

He cleared his throat, spat, and growled. The last remark, I thought, was possibly meant to be a joke. But I was not sure of that. He looked quite capable of carrying out the threat.

He continued. "You've arrived early, which is better than arriving late. We have a cargo to load yet, and in any case it's known that we're not due off for another three days. We can leave a day early, but no more. So the first couple below have got a two-day stint before they see the sky again. Do you want to draw lots for it?"

I glanced at Beanpole. Two days on deck were vastly preferable to spending the time below. But there was the possibility of two days confined with the silent Fritz. Beanpole, his mind presumably working along the same lines, said, "Will and I will volunteer to stay below."

Ulf looked at me, and I nodded. He said, "Just as you like. Show them where they can bunk, Moritz."

A problem that had engaged Beanpole as we came down from the hill to the river bank had been the way in which the barges were propelled. They had no sails, and these, in any case, would have been of limited value in the confines of a river. They could go down, of course, easily enough with the current, but how had they come up to this point against it? As we got nearer, we saw that they had paddle wheels in their sides. Beanpole was excited by the thought that there might be some machine, surviving from the days of the ancients, that moved them.

The truth was disappointing. Each wheel had a treadmill inside, and the treadmill, on journeys upriver, was worked by donkeys. Trained for the task when young, they strained steadily forward and their efforts pulled the barge through the water. It seemed a hard and dreary life, and I was sorry for them, but they were well looked after by Moritz, who was plainly fond of the beasts. They were worked very little on the downriver trips, and were pastured whenever there was an opportunity. They were in a field not far from the river bank now, and would stay there till it was time for the *Erlkönig* to move on. Until they came aboard, Beanpole and I stayed in their small stables, with the smell of donkey and fodder mixing with the smells of old cargoes.

The cargo this time was wooden clocks and carvings. The people who lived in the great forest east of the river made these, and they were shipped downriver to be sold. They had to be loaded with care because of their fragility, and men came aboard the barge to see to this. Beanpole and I hid behind the bales of hay that were kept for the donkeys, and did our best to stay quiet. Once, I could not stop myself from sneezing, but luckily they were talking and laughing loudly enough not to hear it.

But it was a relief when the two days were up and, in the early morning, the barge cast off and moved out into the river. The donkeys worked their treadmill—two at a time, with one resting —and Beanpole and I drew straws for who took

Fritz's place on deck. I won, and went up to a dark, blowy day, with a wind from the north that carried occasional gusts of rain. Yet the air was light and fresh, after my confinement below, and there were many things to be seen on the river and around it. Westward there was a great fertile plain with people working in the fields. To the east the hills stood up, with the black clouds pressing down over their wooded crests. I did not have much time, though, to admire the scenery. Ulf called me and made me get a bucket of water, a brush, and a handful of yellow, soft soap. The decks, he observed truthfully enough, had not been scrubbed for some weeks. I could make myself useful by remedying that.

The progress of the *Erlkönig* was steady, but not fast. In the evening, before it was dark, we tied up on a long island where another barge was already moored. This was one of a number of staging posts that apparently ran the five-hundred-mile length of the river. Moritz explained to me that they were set a distance apart, which was calculated as a minimum day's haul up-river. Going down with the current, one usually covered two stages easily in a day, but to achieve a third meant risking darkness falling before one got there. The barges did not sail by night.

We had seen no sign of Tripods during our journey from the White Mountains through the valleys to the river. During this day on deck, I saw two. Both were distant, striding along the western skyline, three or four miles away at least. But the sight of them gave me a shiver of fear, which took some subduing. For quite long periods it was possible to forget the exact nature of the mission on which we had embarked. Being reminded of it was a nasty jolt.

I tried to console myself with the thought that there had been no hitches so far, that everything was going well. It did not help much, but by the following evening even that small consolation had gone.

The *Erlkönig* stopped at the halfway stage, in a small town, a trading post. Moritz explained that Ulf had some business to conduct there. It would only take him an hour or so, but he had decided, since we were in advance of schedule, to stay over until the following morning. The afternoon lengthened, though, and there was no sign of Ulf returning. Moritz became more and more visibly nervous.

In the end he voiced his apprehensions. Ulf, it seemed, was a man who drank heavily on occasion. Moritz had thought he would not do so on this trip, in view of everything that hung on it, but if the business on which he was engaged had gone wrong and he had become irritated by that, he might have stopped at a tavern, intending to have a drink to soothe his temper, and one thing might have led to another. . . . In a bad bout he might be away from the barge several days.

This was a discouraging thought. The sun dropped down in the west, and there was no Ulf. Moritz began to talk of leaving us on the barge and going in search of him.

The difficulty was that the *Erlkönig*, and Ulf and Moritz, were well known in this town. Already a couple of men had stopped by to offer greetings and chat for a while. If Moritz left, Beanpole would have to handle them (it was his day on deck), and Moritz was unhappy about that. Suspicions might be aroused. They were likely to quiz him in his role as a new apprentice—people on the river were curious about strangers, knowing each other so well—and he might be led into saying something that they would recognize as false.

It was Beanpole who suggested another way. We boys could go and look for Ulf. Choosing moments when no eye was watching, we could slip away in turn, and hunt round the taverns till we found him; then either persuade him to return or, at least, tell Moritz where he was. If we were questioned, we could pass as travelers from far parts: after all, the town was a trading post. It was not the same as having to answer questions about what we were doing on board the *Erlkönig*.

Moritz was dubious, but admitted there was some point in this. Gradually he allowed himself to be persuaded. It was out of the question for all three of us to go searching for Ulf, but one might—Beanpole, since it had been his idea. So Beanpole went, and I at once started working on Moritz to let me go also.

I was helped by the fact that my importunity was matched, on Fritz's part, by indifference. He made no comment and clearly was prepared to wait until things sorted themselves out without assistance from him. So, having allowed one to go, there was only one other for Moritz to consider. I wore him down, as I had known I would; he was more amiable than Ulf, much more amiable, but also less sure of himself. He insisted that I should be back within the hour, whether or not I found Ulf, and I agreed to that. I was tingling with the excitement of exploring a strange town in a strange country. I checked that no one was watching the barge, then jumped quickly onto the quay, and made my way along the waterfront.

It was a bigger place than I had thought, looking at it from the deck of the barge. Fronting the river was a row of warehouses and granaries, many of them with three floors above ground. The buildings were partly of stone but more of wood, and the wood was carved and painted with figures of men and animals. There were a couple of taverns in this stretch, and I looked in briefly, though Beanpole, I guessed, would have covered these before me. One of them was empty, except for two old men, sitting with large mugs of beer (they were called steins, I knew) and smoking pipes. The other had perhaps a dozen men in it, but I could tell in a quick survey that none of them was Ulf.

I came to a road, which ran at right angles to the river, and followed it. There were shops here, and a fair amount of horse traffic, with pony traps and larger carriages and men on horseback. There were, I thought, a lot of people about. I understood why on coming to the first intersection. The crossing road, in either direction, was blocked by stalls that sold food and cloth and all kinds of goods. This was the town's market day.

It was exhilarating, after the long winter of exercise and study in the darkness of the tunnel or on the bare vastness of the mountain side, to be once more among people going about their daily lives. And particularly exhilarating for me, who before fleeing to the White Mountains had known only the quietness of a country village.

A few times I had been taken to Winchester for the market there, and had marveled at it. This town seemed to be as big as Winchester—perhaps even bigger.

I made my way past the stalls. The first was piled high with vegetables: carrots and little potatoes, fat green-and-white spears of asparagus, peas, and huge cabbages, both green and red. At the next there was meat—not simple cuts such as the butcher brought to my village in England, but joints and chops and rolls most delicately decorated with dabs of white lard. I wandered along, gazing and sniffing. One stall was completely given over to cheeses of a score of different colors, shapes, and sizes. I had not realized there could be so many. And a fish stall had dried and smoked fish hanging from hooks and fish fresh caught from the river laid out along a stone slab, their scales still wet. Now, with dusk gathering, some of the stalls were preparing to close down, but most were busy yet, and the press of people, threading their way between and past them, was thick enough.

Between two stalls, one selling leather and the other bolts of cloth, I saw the opening to a tavern, and guiltily remembered what I was supposed to be doing. I went inside and looked about me. It was darker than the taverns on the waterfront, full of tobacco smoke and crowded with dim figures, some sitting at tables and others standing by the bar counter. As I went up to look more closely, I was addressed from the other side of the bar. The speaker was a very big, very fat man, wearing a leather jacket with sleeves of green cloth. In a rough voice, with an accent that I could barely understand, he said, "What is it, then, lad?"

Moritz had given me some coins of the money used in these parts. I did what seemed the safest thing, and ordered a stein of Dunkles, which I knew to be the name of the dark ale that was commonly drunk. The stein was larger than I had expected. He brought it to me, with ale foaming over the side, and I gave him a coin. I drank and had to wipe foam from my lips. It had a bitter sweet taste, which was not unpleasant. I looked round for Ulf, peering into the many dark recesses, whose paneled walls carried the mounted heads of deer and wild boar. I thought for a moment I saw him, but the man moved into the light of an oil lamp, and was a stranger.

I felt nervous. Having a Cap, I was regarded as a man, so that there was no reason why I should not be here. But I lacked the assurance of someone who had been truly Capped, and I was aware, of course, of my difference from all these others. Having established that Ulf was not one of the figures sprawling at the tables, I was eager to be away. As inconspicuously as possible, I put the stein down and began to move toward the street. Before I had gone a couple of paces, the man in the leather jacket roared at me, and I turned back.

"Here!" He pushed over some smaller coins. "You're forgetting your change."

I thanked him, and once more prepared to go. By this time, though, he had seen the stein and that it was two-thirds full.

"You've not drunk your ale, either. Have you got any complaint about it?"

I hastily said no, that it was just that I was not feeling well. To my dismay, I realized that others were taking an interest in me. The man behind the bar seemed partly mollified, but said, "You're not a Württemberger, by the way you talk. Where are you from, then?"

This was a challenge for which I had been prepared. We were to hail from outlying places, in my case a land to the south called Tirol. I told him this.

As far as allaying suspicion was concerned, it worked. From another point of view, though, it was an unfortunate choice. I learned later that there was strong feeling in the town against the Tirol. The previous year at the Games a local champion had been defeated by a Tiroler and, it was claimed, through trickery. One of the others standing by now asked if I were going to the Games, and I incautiously said yes. What followed was a stream of insults. Tirolers were cheats and braggarts, and they spurned good Württemberg ale. They ought to be run out of town, dipped in the river to clean them up a bit . . .

The thing to do was get out, and fast. I stomached the insults and turned to go. Once outside I could lose myself in the crowd. I was thinking of that and did not look closely enough in front of me. A leg was stretched out from one of the tables and, to the accompaniment of a roar of laughter, I went sprawling in the sawdust that covered the floor.

Even that I was prepared to endure, though I had banged one knee painfully as I landed. I began to get to my feet. As I did so, fingers gripped the hair that grew up through my Cap, shook my head violently to and fro, and thrust me down once more to the ground.

I should have been thankful that this assault had not dislodged the false Cap and exposed me. I should also have been concentrating on what really mattered—getting away from here and safely and unnoticed back to the barge. But I am afraid that I could think of nothing but the pain and humiliation. I got up again, saw a face grinning behind me, and swung at him in fury.

He was probably a year or so older than I was, and bigger and heavier. He fended me off contemptuously. My mind did not cool down enough for me to realize how stupidly I was behaving, but enough for the skills I had acquired during my long training to take over. I feinted toward him and, as he swung a still casual arm in my direction, slipped inside and belted him hard over the heart. Now it was his turn to go sprawling, and there was a roar from the men crowding round us. He got up slowly, his face angry. The others moved back, forming a ring, clearing the tables to do so. I realized I had to go through with it. I was not afraid of that, but I could appreciate my own folly. I had been warned about my rashness by Julius, and now, within a week of starting out on an enterprise of such desperate importance, it had already betrayed me.

He rushed at me, and I had to concern myself again with what was present and immediate. I sidestepped and hit him as he went past. Although he was bigger than I was, he was lacking in skill. I could have danced round him for as long as I liked, cutting him to pieces. But that would not do at all. What was needed was one disabling blow. From every point of view, the sooner this was over the better.

So the next time he attacked I rode his punch with my left shoulder, sank my right fist into the vulnerable area just under his ribs, and, stepping back, caught him with as powerful a left hook as I could manage as, gulping air, his head involuntarily came forward. I got a lot of strength into it. He went backward even faster and hit the floor. The men watching were silent. I looked at my fallen opponent and, seeing that he showed no signs of getting up, moved in the direction of the door, expecting that the ring would open to let me through.

But that did not happen. They stared at me sullenly without budging. One of them knelt beside the prone figure.

He said, "He hit his head. He may be hurt badly."

Someone else said, "You ought to get the police."

A few hours later I stared up at the stars, bright in a clear black sky. I was cold and hungry, miserable and disgusted with myself. I was a prisoner in the Pit.

I had met very rough justice at the hands of the magistrate who had examined me. The fellow I had knocked out was a nephew of his, a son of a leading merchant in the town. The evidence was that I had provoked him in the tavern

by saying things derogatory of the Württem-
bergers, and that I had then hit him when he
was not looking. It bore no resemblance at all
to what had happened, but there were a number
of witnesses who agreed on the story. My opponent, to give him possible credit, was not one
of these, the reason being that he had suffered a
concussion when his head hit the floor. He was
in no state to say anything to anybody. I was
warned that if he failed to recover I would as-
suredly be hanged. Meanwhile I was to be con-
signed to the Pit, during the magistrate's pleasure.

This was their preferred way of dealing with
malefactors. The Pit was round, some fifteen
feet across and about as many feet deep. The
floor was of rough flagstones, and the walls were
also lined with stones. They were smooth
enough to discourage attempts at climbing up,
and there were iron spikes near the top, projecting inward, which further discouraged thoughts
of escape. I had been dropped over these like a
sack of potatoes, and left. I had been given no
food, and had nothing to cover me in a night
that looked as though it was going to be cold. I
had banged my elbow and grazed my arm in the
fall.

But the real fun, as I had been told with satisfaction by some of my captors, would take place

the following day. The Pit was designed partly
for punishment, partly for the amusement of the
local people. It was their custom to stand at the
top and pelt the unfortunate prisoner with whatever came to hand or mind. Filth of all kinds—
rotting vegetables, slops, that sort of thing—
were what they chiefly preferred, but if they
were really annoyed they might use stones, bil-
lets of wood, or broken bottles. In the past pris-
oners had sometimes been severely injured,
even killed. They appeared to get a lot of pleasure out of the prospect, and out of telling me
about it.

I supposed it was something that the skies
had cleared. There was no protection here from
the elements. By the wall was a trough with
water in it. Although I was thirsty, I was not yet
thirsty enough to drink it; there had been
enough light, when I was first thrown down, to
see that it was covered by a greenish scum. No
food was provided to those in the Pit. When
they got sufficiently hungry they would eat the
rotting refuse, bones, and stale bread that were
hurled at them. That, too, was supposed to be
amusing.

What a fool I had been. I shivered, and cursed
my idiocy, and shivered again.

Gradually the night wore through. A couple
of times I lay down, curled myself up, and tried
to sleep. But it was growing colder, and I had to

get up again and walk about to restore my circulation. I longed for the day and dreaded it at the same time. I wondered what had happened to the others—whether Ulf had got back yet. I knew there was no hope of him intervening on my behalf. He was quite well known in this town, but he dared not take the risk of associating with me. Tomorrow they would go downriver, leaving me here. There was nothing else they could do.

The wide circle of sky above me brightened, and I could tell which side faced east by the softer light there. For a change, I sat with my back to the stone wall. Tiredness, despite the cold, crept over me. My head nodded to my chest. Then a sound overhead jerked me into wakefulness. I saw a face peering down. It was a small silhouette against the paling dawn. An early riser, I thought drearily, impatient to get at the victim. It would not be long before the throwing started.

Then a voice called quietly down.

"Will—are you all right?"

Beanpole's voice.

He had brought a length of rope from the barge. He stretched down and tied it to one of the iron spikes, then tossed the other end to me. I grabbed it, and hauled myself up. The spikes took some negotiating, but Beanpole was able to get a hand over them to help me. In a matter of seconds, I was heaving myself and being hauled over the edge of the Pit.

We wasted no time in discussing our situation. The Pit was on the outskirts of the town, which, sleeping still but outlined now in the clear light of dawn, stood between us and the place where the *Erlkönig* was moored. I had only a hazy recollection of being brought here the previous evening, but Beanpole ran confidently and I followed him. It took us perhaps ten minutes to come within sight of the river, and we had seen only one man, in the distance, who shouted something but did not attempt to follow our fleeing figures. Beanpole, I realized, had timed things perfectly. We passed the street where the market had been. In another fifty yards we should be on the quay.

We reached it and turned left. About as far again along, just past the tavern, next to the barge called *Siegfried*, I stared and stopped, and Beanpole did the same. The *Siegfried* was there all right, but the berth next to her was empty.

Beanpole, after a moment, plucked my sleeve. I looked where he indicated, in the opposite direction, to the north. The *Erlkönig* was out in midstream, beating downriver, a quarter of a mile off, a toy boat rapidly diminishing in the distance.

3

A Raft
on the
River

Our first concern was to get away before my escape from the Pit became known. We went north along the waterfront, through a few mean streets with ramshackle buildings quite unlike the painted, carved, and well-cared-for houses in the center of the town, and found a road—little better than a track—that followed the general line of the river. The sun rose on our right, behind the wooded hills. There were clouds there, too, forming with ominous speed. Within half an hour they had darkened the sky and blanked out the sun; in three quarters, a gray belt of rain was sweeping down the slope toward us. Five minutes later, already soaking wet, we found shelter in a ruined building lying back from the road. We had time then to think over what had happened, and what we should do about it.

On the way, Beanpole had told me his side of events. He had not found Ulf, but when he returned to the barge Ulf was there. He *had* been drinking, and it had not improved his temper. He was furious with Beanpole and me for having gone into the town, and with Moritz for having allowed us. We two, he had decided, would spend the remainder of the trip down-river below decks. Fritz, obviously, was the only one who could be relied on, the only one with any sense.

As time passed without my return, his anger increased. After dark, one of the men he knew, coming to see him, spoke of the young Tiroler who had started a fracas in a tavern, and who in consequence had been condemned to the Pit. When this man had gone, Ulf spoke in a more coldly angry and implacable fashion. My folly had jeopardized everything. I was clearly a liability to the enterprise, rather than an asset. There was to be no more waiting, and certainly no attempt to set me free. In the morning the *Erlkönig* would resume its voyage. It would take two participants to the Games instead of three. As far as I was concerned, I had got myself into the Pit and I could stay there and rot.

Although he did not talk about it, I know that Beanpole found himself cruelly in a quandary over this. We were under Ulf's authority, and ought to obey him in all things. Moreover, what he said was entirely reasonable. Above all, it was the project itself that mattered, not individuals. His job was to do his best to win at the Games, to gain entry into the City of the Tripods, and to bring out of it information that might help to destroy them. That was what was really important.

But Beanpole talked to Moritz, asking him questions particularly about the Pit: what it was like, where it was situated. I do not know whether Moritz was too stupid to see where the questions might be tending, or whether he understood and approved. He was, I thought, really too amiable a man for work that, of its nature, required a streak of ruthlessness. Anyway, Beanpole found out what he wanted to know and, at first light, took a length of rope and left the *Erlkönig* in search of me. Presumably Ulf heard or saw something of his departure and either in rage or out of cold logic decided there was nothing to do but salvage the one reliable member of the trio and get the *Erlkönig* under way before there could be any question of suspicion falling on the boat or its crew.

So here we were, stranded, hundreds of miles short of our objective.

The rain stopped as abruptly as it had started, and gave way to hot sunlight in which our wet clothes steamed as we walked. We were drenched again less than an hour later—this time there was no shelter at all and the torrential downpour soaked us to our skins—and the day proved to be one of sunburst and cloudburst. Most of the time we were sodden and miserable; all the time we were conscious of the mess we—and I in particular—had made of things.

We were also hungry. I had eaten nothing since the previous midday, and as soon as the immediate excitement of escape and flight had died down, I was aware of ravenous hunger. We had what was left of the money we had got from Moritz, but there was nowhere to spend it out in the open country, and we had not fancied waiting in the town until the shops opened. The land through which we were traveling was either waste or pasture, with groups of black-

and-white cows chewing their cuds. I proposed
milking one, and with Beanpole's assistance
cornered her in an angle of a field. But it was a
fiasco. I got out no more than a few drops. She
objected strongly to my rough and inexperienced
handling and forced her way clear. It did not
seem worthwhile trying again.

Several hours after we started, we came on a
turnip field. There was a cottage within sight of
it, but we risked taking some. They were small
and bitter, but it was something to chew on. The
rain came down again as we continued, and this
time lasted without ceasing for an hour or more.

We found a patch of ruins in which to spend
the night. We had discovered no other source
of food, and chewed grass and the green shoots
of the hedgerow in an attempt to stay our hunger.
It was ineffective, and gave us stomach pains.
Also, of course, our clothes were wet. We tried
to sleep but with poor success. We were awake
as night grayed into morning, and set off, tired
and wretched, on our way.

It did not actually rain, but the day was
cloudy and chilling. The river rolled beside us,
broad and turbulent, and we watched a barge
go downstream and thought we detected, in its
wake, the fragrance of bacon frying on the gal-
ley stove. Not far on, we found a cluster of
houses, a farming hamlet. Beanpole had the

idea of presenting himself as a Vagrant, hoping to be given food. I offered to do it instead, but he said it was his idea, and I must keep out of sight: Vagrants never traveled in company. So I hid in a hedge, and watched.

In my village at home there had been the Vagrant House, provided for the use of these poor wandering madmen. There they were given food and drink, and there were servants to clean and cook. Beanpole had told me that in his country nothing of this sort was provided. Vagrants slept rough and where they could—in barns if they were lucky, or in ruins. They begged their food from door to door, and it was given them with varying generosity.

We had assumed that something of the sort might apply here. There were half a dozen houses, and I saw Beanpole go up to the first of them and knock at the door. It did not open; later he told me that a voice from inside shouted at him to go away, adding curses. At the second door there was no response at all. At the third, a window opened and a bucket of dirty water was thrown over him, to the accompaniment of laughter. As he went away, wetter than before, the door opened. He half turned, prepared to put up with insults if there was a chance of food, and then fled. They had loosed a savage-looking brindle dog on him. It chased him halfway to where I was lying and then stood barking its hostility after him.

Half a mile farther on we found and raided a potato field. They were small, and would have been more palatable cooked. But we had no prospect of making a fire in this cold, gray sullen land. We slogged on and, as darkness fell, saw ahead of us downriver a barge moored by the bank. I think the same thought struck us both: that it might be the *Erlkönig*, that for some reason Ulf might have been held up and that we might rejoin them. It was an absurd hope, but it was bitter, all the same, to have it dashed. The barge was bigger than the *Erlkönig*, and was making upstream, not down. We went away from the river to circle past it.

Later we came back to the river bank, to sit shivering in a broken-down hut. An unhappy silence had fallen. I wondered if Beanpole was thinking that he might but for me have been safe and warm and well-fed on the barge. I thought about that myself, though it did no good.

Then he said, "Will."

"Yes."

"Where the barge was moored, there was a wharf, and a couple of houses. That would be one of the stages."

"I suppose so."

"The first we have passed since the town."

I thought about that. "Yes. Yes, it is."

"Ulf was reckoning to cover two stages a day, taking things easily. So in two days . . ."

In two days we had covered a distance the barge would have sailed in a morning, though we had walked from first light till it was too dark to see where we were going. It was reasonable enough, but discouraging. I made no comment.

Beanpole went on, "It was planned that we should get there three days before the opening of the Games. It was to take five days. At this rate, we shall take twenty. The Games will be over before we arrive."

"Yes." I tried to rouse myself from torpor. "Do you think we ought to go back instead?"

"To the tunnel? I don't like to think what we should say to Julius in that case."

Nor did I, but I did not see what else we could do.

Beanpole said, "We must get on faster. There is the river."

"We dare not approach one of the other barges. You know what was said about that. They're suspicious of strangers and never allow them on board."

"If we had a boat of our own . . ."

"It would be a fine thing," I said, with a touch,

I fear, of sarcasm. "Or if we found a Shmand-Fair traveling along the river bank and could climb aboard it."

Beanpole said patiently, "A boat—or a raft? The side of this hut, maybe? It is falling apart, as it is. If we could detach it, and get it into the water . . . the current would carry us twice as fast as we could walk at least, and much more directly."

I took his point, and felt a sudden unexpected lift of hope, which for a moment allowed me to forget my cold shivering limbs and groaning empty stomach. It just might be possible. Long ago as a boy I had helped to make a raft under the supervision of my cousin Jack, and we had floated it on a nearby duck pond. It had collapsed and precipitated us into pea-soup water and stinking mud. But we had been children then. This was a different proposition.

I said, "Do you think we can . . . ?"

"In the morning," Beanpole said. "We will try in the morning."

The day, as though to encourage us, started bright. We tackled the job at first light. It was encouragingly easy, and then discouragingly difficult. The wall Beanpole had spoken of was about six feet square, and already largely split away from the roof. We completed the separation and freed the sides. After that it was simple enough to press it outward and down. It collapsed with a satisfying clatter—and in several sections, as the individual planks fell apart.

The thing to do, Beanpole said, was to secure them with cross pieces. Planks taken from the other walls would do. As for the means of securing them, we would have to take nails out and drive them in again where needed. He spoke with a fine practical-sounding confidence.

The trouble was that most of the existing nails were both twisted and rusted, in some cases to the point where they broke under simple finger pressure. We had to hunt for reasonably sound ones, to lever them out carefully, avoiding any further distortion, and then straighten them and drive them through the crossed planks. We had nothing like a hammer, of course. We had to use chunks of stone with fairly flat surfaces. Beanpole found quite a good one and surrendered it to me because, as he said, I could use it better. This was true. I have always been fairly skilled with my hands—more so, I am afraid, than with my head.

It was hard work and took time. We were sweating by the time we finished, and the sun stood clear above the hills. That left us with the task of getting our raft into the water, and this was not easy, either. The hut was some fifty

"The river . . ." I said. "It must fork there."

"Yes," Beanpole said. "Will, I think we must swim for it now."

I had learned to swim in the rivers around my village of Wherton, and once or twice, illicitly, in the lake up at the estate. It was better than nothing, but Beanpole had grown up in a seaside town. He pulled away from me with powerful strokes, realized I was falling behind, and called out, "Are you all right?"

I called back doggedly, "All right," and concentrated on swimming. The current was very strong. The shore at which I was aiming slid past and behind. Only gradually did I make an impression on the distance. Then I saw something that dismayed me. Ahead the shore became a spit, with a wider reach of water beyond it. This was not a place where the river forked, but an island. If I missed it, there was the wider passage ahead. Already tired, I would find myself in midstream with a much longer haul to come. I altered course and swam almost directly against the current. I heard Beanpole call again, but could not spare the energy to look for him or to reply. I struggled on, my arms becoming more and more leaden, the water colder and fiercer and more implacable. I no longer looked where I was heading, concerned only with forcing my arms into and out of the water. Then something hit my head and I went under, dazed. I remembered nothing after that until I was aware of someone dragging me, and of firm ground under my feet.

It was Beanpole who pulled me up onto a grassy bank. When I had recovered enough to take in my surroundings, I saw by how small a margin we had made it. We were within a few yards of the northernmost limit of the island. It lay in the center of the river's bend, and just ahead the river broadened considerably. My head was hurting, and I put my hand up to my forehead.

"A plank hit you," Beanpole said. "From the raft, I think. How do you feel, Will?"

"A bit dizzy," I said. Something else returned. "And hungry. Across there—isn't it . . . ?"

"Yes," he said, "a village."

Despite the deepening dusk, it was possible to see houses on the east bank. Some had lights in their windows. By this time I would have been prepared to take a chance on having dirty water thrown over me or being chased by large dogs—even on being questioned as to what I was doing here—but not on trusting myself to the river again. I could think more clearly, but physically I was as weak as though I had spent a month in bed.

"We will get across there in the morning," Beanpole said.

"Yes," I nodded wearily, "in the morning."

"The trees are thicker farther back. More shelter, if it rains."

I nodded again, and moved my leaden legs forward for a few steps only, and then stopped. Someone was standing by the edge of the trees, watching us. When he realized we had seen him, he came toward us. In the dim light I could see that he was a man in his middle years, tall and lean, dressed in rough-looking dark trousers and shirt, his hair long and his face bearded. I saw something else, too. Although his hair hung down behind his neck, it receded at the forehead. It was dark hair, beginning to turn gray. And where the silver band of the Cap should have been there was only flesh, toughened and browned by long years of exposure.

He spoke in German, in a harsh dialect. He had been looking out and had seen us struggling in the water, and had watched Beanpole haul me in to shore. His manner was odd, I thought— part grudging and part welcoming. I had the feeling that he would have been quite happy to see us drift on past, and would not have spared more than a moment's thought for our chances of escaping drowning. But now that we were here . . .

He said, "You'll want to dry yourselves out. You'd better come with me."

All sorts of questions were in my mind, apart from the really crucial one of why he was not one of the Capped. But it seemed best to do as he said and let enlightenment wait. I looked at Beanpole and he nodded. The man led the way to what I saw was a well-trodden path. It wound between the trees for several minutes before coming out into a clearing. In front of us there was a wooden hut, with an oil lamp burning in the window and smoke blowing from its chimney. He unlatched the door and went inside, we following.

A log fire was burning in a stone fireplace. There was a large woolen rug in front of it—red with weirdly shaped black and yellow animals—and sitting on the rug were three cats. Two of them were tabbies, marked with white patches, the third an oddly patterned black and white with a white face and a funny black moustache under the nose. The man moved them with his foot, not roughly, but merely forcing them to yield their place. He went to a cupboard and produced two lengths of coarse toweling.

"Get your wet things off," he said. "Warm yourselves in front of the fire. I've got a couple of shirts and trousers you can put on while your own are drying." He stared at us fiercely. "Are you hungry?"

We looked at each other. Beanpole said, "Very hungry, sir. If you . . ."

"Don't call me sir. I'm Hans. Bread and cold ham. I don't usually cook at night."

"Just bread will do," I said.

"Aye," he said. "You look starved. Get yourselves dry, then."

The trousers and shirt were too big, of course, particularly in my case. I had to roll the bottoms up and he gave me a belt to put round the middle. I was lost inside the shirt. While we were changing, he had been putting things on a scrubbed wooden table under the window: a couple of knives, plates, a dish of yellow butter, a large flat loaf of brown bread, and a ham, partly cut, that showed firm pink meat surrounded by clear white fat, baked brown on the outside. I sliced into it, while Beanpole cut bread. I saw Hans watching me, and was a little ashamed of the thickness of the slices I was cutting. But he nodded, approvingly. He brought over a couple of mugs, plonked them by our plates, and returned with a big earthenware jar from which he poured us dark draughts of beer. We set to. I warned myself to eat slowly, but to no avail. The ham was sweet and good, the bread nutty and coarse-textured, the butter of a finer quality than I had tasted since leaving home. The beer with which I washed it down was strong and sweet. My jaws ached with chewing, but my belly still clamored for nourishment.

Hans said, "You were hungry, all right." I looked guiltily at my plate. "Never mind. Eat on. I like to see someone enjoying his victuals."

I ground to a halt at last; Beanpole had finished much earlier. I was feeling full, in fact overfull, and happy. The room was snug, with the glow of lamplight and the flicker of firelight and the three cats, back in their original positions, purring away in the hearth. I presumed that now we would be asked questions: where we had come from, the reason for our being in the river. But this did not happen. Our host sat in a wooden rocking chair that looked as though he might have made it himself, and smoked a pipe. He did not seem to find silence awkward or constraining. In the end, it was Beanpole who said, "Could you tell us how it is that you are not Capped?"

Hans took his pipe from his mouth. "I've never bothered."

"Not bothered!"

It came out slowly, through prodding from both of us. His father had brought him to this island as a young boy after his mother died. The pair of them had lived together here, growing their own vegetables, keeping chickens and a few pigs, making things to sell in the village across the river. Then his father had died, in turn, and he had stayed on. No one from the village troubled about him; he was not counted as part of their life. This happened in the spring of the year in which he would have been Capped, and during that summer he had not moved from the island, concerned only with doing on his own all the things in which previously he had assisted his father. (He had buried his father, he told us, not far from the hut, and over slow months that winter carved a stone with his name to put over his grave.) Since then he had gone across to the village perhaps twice a year. He had a boat in which he rowed there and back.

At first I was incredulous, thinking of the trouble we who had fled to the White Mountains had taken to avoid being Capped, while this man had just stayed where he was, not worrying. Surely there could not be flaws like this in the Tripods' mastery of the earth? But the more I thought about it, the less surprising it seemed. He was one man, living like a hermit. The domination of the Tripods depended on the serfdom of men as such, and to that end it was enough that Capping should be accepted as a natural and inevitable thing where a handful of men, two or three even, were gathered together. One man did not matter, as long as he stayed quiet and caused no trouble. And the moment he did cause trouble, of course, he would be dealt with, either by the Tripods or their human servants. There would be no difficulty in that.

Beanpole, once he had established all this, quizzed him about the Tripods. Did he see much of them? What did he feel about them? I saw where the line of questioning was heading, and was content to leave it to him. He did not seem surprised at or suspicious of the conversation, and this in itself showed how small his contact with the wider world must have been. Local customs varied in different countries, but in every one the subject of Tripods and Caps was covered by a taboo. No one, Capped as we appeared to be, would have spoken like this.

But if unsuspicious, he was also indifferent. He saw the Tripods from time to time, yes. He believed they damaged crops on the mainland; it was hard to see how they could avoid it, great massive things that they were. But none of them, he was glad to say, had ever planted its heavy foot on this island. As for Caps, well, people wore them, and they didn't seem to do a lot of harm and didn't seem to do any particular good. He believed it was something to do with the Tripods, since the boys who went for Capping were taken up by the Tripods. Did they prevent people wanting to fight against the Tripods, Beanpole asked daringly.

Hans looked at him over his pipe. He said shrewdly, "Well, you'd know more about that than I do, would you not? But it wouldn't make a lot of sense wanting to fight against the Tripods, would it? You would have to be pretty strong in the arm to throw a stone high enough to hit that part at the top, and what good would it do you if you did? For that matter, what's the point in it? It's not as though they do any harm. A bit of damage now and then to crops and cattle—to men, maybe; if they don't get out of the way fast enough. But lightning can kill you with even less chance of dodging, and hailstones can ruin crops."

Beanpole said, "We were on a raft farther up the river. The raft was smashed by a Tripod. That's how we came to be washed up here."

Hans nodded. "Bad luck comes to everyone. Some sickness got among my hens two years back. Wiped out all but three of them."

"We're very grateful to you," Beanpole said, "for giving us food and shelter."

Hans stared from his face to the fire, and back. "As to that, I get along without seeing people well enough, but now you're here. . . . There's some wood that needs cutting, up at the top end. I've had rheumatics in my shoulder, and it's not got done. You can get on with that tomorrow, and it will pay for the food you eat, and your lodging. Later, maybe, I'll row you across to the village."

Beanpole started to say something then stopped and merely nodded. There was silence again, Hans staring into the fire. I said, part exasperated, part in hope, "But if you found people who were fighting against the Tripods— wouldn't you help them? After all, you are a free man."

He looked at me for some moments before replying. "That's strange talk," he said. "I don't have a lot to do with people, but it sounds strange talk to me. You don't come from these parts, lad."

It was part accusation, part question. I said, "But if there *were* men who were not slaves of the Tripods, surely you would want to do what you could . . ."

I found my voice trailing off under the steady regard of the bearded man.

"Strange talk," he repeated. "I mind my own business. I always have, and I always will. Are you one of those they call Vagrants, maybe? But they travel around by themselves, not in couples. I don't have trouble with anyone, because I keep out of it. You seem to want to start trouble. If that's the way you think . . ."

Beanpole cut in on him. He said, with a quick look of warning at me beforehand, "You mustn't pay any attention to him, Hans. He's feeling queer. When he was in the water he was hit on the head by one of the planks from the raft. You can see the bruise on his forehead."

Hans got up from his feet, and came toward me. He peered at my head for a long time. Then he said. "Aye. He's maybe addled his wits a bit. It won't hinder him from swinging an ax in the morning. But you'll both benefit from a good night's sleep. I rise early, so I don't stay up late."

He brought blankets from the hut's other room, in which he slept. Then, with a gruff goodnight, he left us, taking the lamp with him. Beanpole and I settled ourselves down on the floor, on either side of the fire. I was feeling vaguely uncomfortable from the supper, which, following the previous two days' privation, was not proving easy to digest. I expected to have a restless night. But tiredness was stronger than queasiness. I looked at the glow of the fire and the three cats still sentinel in front of it. My next sight was of sunlight on cold ashes, the cats gone, and Hans, whose heavy tread had wakened me, calling to us to get up.

The breakfast he prepared for us was enormous. Great slices of grilled gammon with as many eggs as we wanted (I ate three), and hot, golden-brown potato cakes. With it we drank more of the beer he had given us the previous night.

"Eat well," Hans said. "The more you eat, the better you'll work."

He took us with him to the north of the island. There was a field of about an acre, under potatoes, and he explained that he wanted to extend it by cutting down and rooting out the trees in the adjoining copse. He had started this task, but the rheumatism in his shoulder had first hindered and then entirely prevented him. He provided us with an ax, spade, and mattock, watched us while we set to, and left us.

It was hard work. The sap was rising in the trees and the roots of those already cut down were tangled and hard to dig out. Beanpole suggested that, if we worked hard, he might regard a morning's work as sufficient return for hospitality and take us across the river in the afternoon. But although we sweated at the job, the going proved slow. When Hans came for us, toward midday, he looked critically at our results.

"I thought you would have done better than that. Still, you've made a start. You'd better come now for your dinner."

He had roasted a couple of chickens, and he served these with a heap of buttered potatoes and a sour-tasting cabbage. He gave us wine with it because drinking beer in the middle of the day, he said, was likely to make us sluggish. Afterward there were sweet blueberries doused with cream. Then he said, "You can rest now for half an hour, and digest your food, while I get things cleared up. Then you get back to the field. Leave that big oak till tomorrow. I want to make sure she falls the right way."

He left us lying in the sun. I said to Beanpole, "Tomorrow? So much for him offering to take us across the river this afternoon."

Beanpole said slowly, "Tomorrow, and the day after, and the day after that. He is determined to keep us here until the wood is cleared."

"But that would take a week, at least, probably two!"

Beanpole said, "Yes. And we have little time if we are to compete in the Games."

"We shall not manage that, anyway, on foot. We should have to find the material for another raft, and build it. And even then I doubt if we could do it. We need a boat."

I stopped as an idea struck me, surprised that it had not occurred to me before. We had seen Hans's boat on our way up to the field. It was tied in a small inlet on the east of the island, a sturdy-looking six-footer, with a pair of oars.

Beanpole, from the look he gave me, was clearly thinking along the same lines.

I said, "If we managed to slip away this evening . . . I suppose it would be a pretty rotten trick, but . . ."

"The boat must mean a great deal to him," Beanpole said. "He depends on it to get to and from the village. I think probably he built it himself, or his father did, and it would take him a long time to build another, particularly with the pain in his shoulder. But we know from what he said last night that he would never help us, although he is not Capped. He would keep us here, working for him, even if he knew what our mission was. I think getting into the City is more important, Will, than this lonely old man and his boat."

"So, this evening . . ."

"This evening loses us half a day, and there may not be another time when we know ourselves to be unwatched." He rose to his feet. "I think now is better."

We walked in as innocent a manner as possible toward the shelter of the trees. As we approached them, I glanced back and saw the open door of the hut, but no sign of Hans. We went more quickly after that, running in the direction of the inlet and the boat. It rocked as Beanpole climbed aboard and unshipped the oars, while I saw to the rope that tied it to the branch of a tree. It was tied in a complicated knot, over which I struggled with, at first, little effect.

Beanpole said, "Hurry, Will."

"If I had a knife . . ."

"I think I hear someone."

I heard it, too—running feet and now a voice, calling harshly. I wrenched desperately at the knot, and it came free. Then I scrambled into the boat, which tilted dangerously under us. As Beanpole pushed off from the bank, the figure of Hans burst through from the trees, shouting curses. We were ten feet clear by the time he reached the water's edge. He did not stop but plunged in after us. The fast-flowing water came up to his knees, then his thighs, but he waded on, still cursing. Where it reached his waist, he succeeded in grasping at the blade of one of the oars, but Beanpole pulled it from him. The current took us, and we moved out toward midstream.

Hans fell silent then, and his expression changed. I had borne his earlier raving and anger easily enough, but this was different. I still feel sick when I remember the terrible despair in his face.

We went downriver swiftly enough after that. We took turns at the oars, started early, and rowed until late each day. Food was a problem, but we managed, although after the first day we were hungry all the time. We passed barges, traveling upstream and down, and kept clear of them, which was increasingly easy as the great river broadened on its course to the sea. The river itself was a source of great interest, rolling through varied scenery, woods, pasture, vineyards, and wheatfields, and the silent, somber heaps, mounded up on either side, of the ruined cities of the ancients. We saw Tripods many times, and once heard the wild warbling of their hunting call, but that was far in the distance. None approached us closely. There were rivers that ran in to join the mother river, castles of great antiquity lifted high on spurs of cliff, and in one place a huge tawny mass of tree-decked rock, taller than a Tripod, set in midstream.

Finally we came to where the Games were held. There were many barges tied up there, the *Erlkönig* among them.

5

The
Games

It was a land of flower-starred meadows, heavy, rich-yielding earth, small prosperous villages, and windmills everywhere, their sails turning slowly in warm gusts of wind. The season was perhaps not so far advanced as in the south, but the weather seemed to have set in fair. This was true Games weather, people said, though I thought the fact that so many of them remarked on it might indicate that true Games weather was more a rarity than a reasonable expectation.

The town lay west of the river, behind meadows that, as we made our way through them, were hot and slumbrous in the afternoon sun. Many people were traveling that way, not only competitors but spectators to see the Games. The town and nearby villages seemed to bulge with them, and thousands more set up tents in the fields. There was an air of festival—much eating and drinking of beer and last year's wine, everyone, it seemed, happy, and dressed in their best. We had got there the day before the opening. That night we had to sleep where best we could—in the open, as it proved, under willow trees beside a rushing stream—but tomorrow, providing we passed the early trials and were accepted, we would be competitors and be housed in the long, low wooden huts built near the Field.

To reach that place one passed through the town, with its great twin-towered church and its newly painted houses, and skirted the hill that looked down on it. (Wandering there once, we found a vast semicircular pit, descending in levels faced with stone to a central stone platform. We could not guess its purpose, but the stones were cracked and worn and distorted by what must have been not years but centuries. And all those centuries, I thought, before the coming of the Tripods—generation on generation.) Beyond was a village and nearby, the Field. It was huge, and the local people told a story of it. In the days of the ancients, they said, there had been many great battles, in which— though it was scarcely to be believed—men had slaughtered each other because of their wickedness. This was the field of the last, most immense and savage battle of all, though where some said it had happened, others believed it was still to take place. Hearing this, I hoped it was an omen for our success. One battle needed to be fought, and we, here, were the outriders of our army.

We had seen Moritz at the barge, but not Ulf, who was off drinking. Moritz was pleased to see us, but urged us not to stay because Ulf's anger was still strong and not likely to be much appeased by our having got here in time after all. Fritz, he told us, had gone up to the Field that morning.

There were flags and banners in all the towns and villages, and they surrounded the Field like the fluttering petals of a thousand huge and gaudy flowers. Behind and above were the tiers of wood on which people sat and watched, with peddlers moving among them selling trinkets and ribbons, sweetmeats, wine, and hot sausages. Projecting from one side was the judges' pavilion, with a dais in front to which the winners would come to claim their champions' belts. To which, we fervently hope, we would go.

On the first day, as I have said, those who were obviously unsuitable were weeded out. We had not felt any doubt that we should qualify, and we did so easily. I was set to box with a boy of roughly my own age and weight, and in less than a minute the judge broke off the bout and sent me to be weighed and entered. I met Fritz again in the tent, which had been set aside for these procedures. He showed neither surprise at my appearance nor curiosity as to how I had got here. I told him Beanpole was here, too, and he nodded. Three chances were better than one. I had the notion, though, that all along he had believed that it was he who would succeed in getting into the City—that we were not to be relied on. I almost hoped that he would lose in his first race, but checked myself in my stupid resentment. What mattered was that one of us should succeed, and as he said, better three than one.

Later I found Beanpole again. He, also, had qualified without difficulty, clearing the required distance in both jumps by an easy margin. We went together to the dining tent for our midday meal; we were given our food, as well as a bed. I asked him how he felt about his chances now that the challenge was on us. He said seriously,

"All right, I think. I did not have to try hard. And you, Will?"

"The one I beat has qualified, too. I saw him in the hut."

"That sounds good. Do you think we ought to look for Fritz?"

"There'll be time, later. Let's eat first."

Next morning was the opening ceremony. People came in procession from the town, carrying the banners of the Games, and the Games Captain, an old white-haired man who was the leader of the officials, made a speech of welcome to the contestants assembled on the Field, full of phrases about sportsmanship and honor. I might have been impressed if it were not for those others who were also present. During the tournament at the Château de la Tour Rouge, one Tripod had stood above the castle, in silent scrutiny of events. Here there were six. They had marched in early in the morning and were already present, lined up round the Field, when we awoke. Words like sportsmanship and honor had a hollow sound when one remembered that the purpose of these sports was to provide slaves for these metal monsters. Slaves, or sacrifices. After all, though hundreds of men and women each year entered the City, none had yet been known to come out. Thinking of that, I shivered despite the warmth of the sun.

There was no boxing on that day, and I was able to watch the preliminaries in the other events. Fritz was entered for the hundred- and two-hundred-meters races. These were popular events: for the first there were to be twelve heats, ten entrants in each, with the first and second runners going through to three further races in which the first three qualified. Fritz came in second in the fourth heat. This could have been misleading, of course, but it looked to me as though he were straining hard. The first part of the long jump was held in the afternoon, and Beanpole won easily, half a meter ahead of his nearest rival.

My own first trial came the following morning. My opponent was a tall, skinny lad, who moved quickly but was almost entirely defensive. I chased him round the ring, missing occasionally but landing punches more often, and had no doubt about the result. Later in the day I fought again, and again won easily. Beanpole had been watching. Afterward I put on the track suit they had given me, and we went to watch the field events. The two-hundred-meters heats were being run. Beanpole strained his eyes toward the announcement board, but had to ask me which race had been reached. I told him seven.

"Then Fritz has already run," he said. "His heat was six. Are the results up?"

"They're going up now."

The results board was to one side of the judges' pavilion. It had an elaborate system of trapdoors and ladders and ledges behind it through which a troup of boys put up the numbers of the winners. The numbers of the two qualifiers in heat six appeared on the board while I watched.

Beanpole said, "Well?"

I shook my head. "No."

Beanpole made no comment, nor did I. Fritz's elimination from one of his two events was our first defeat, forcing us to the realization that there might be others. It would be sickening if we were all forced back, defeated, from this first obstacle, but the possibility had to be reckoned with.

For me, personally, the possibility became very real the next time I fought. This opponent, like the first, was fast, but he was more skilled and much more aggressive. In the initial round he landed several good punches, and made me miss when I counterattacked, once leaving me tangled with the ropes. I had no doubt in my mind that I had lost the round, and was in a fair way to losing the contest. When we came out again I concentrated on getting in close and punching to the body. I did better, but I had a feeling I was still behind on points. I went into the last round in a desperate mood. I attacked in a fury that rattled my opponent. He opened up his guard and I caught him with a right to the side of the head, which floored him. He got up at once, but he was nervous after that and tried to keep his distance. He was also plainly tiring, probably from the body blows in the previous round.

I was confident, by the time the final bell went, that I had made up lost ground, but I could not be sure how much. I saw the three judges conferring together. They were taking longer than usual about it, and my uncertainty and apprehension curdled into physical sickness. I was trembling when we went back to the center of the ring, and could scarcely believe it when the referee lifted my arm in the sign of victory.

Fritz and Beanpole had both been watching. Beanpole said, "I thought you were going to lose that one."

I was still feeling shaky, but with relief now. I said, "So did I."

"You left it late," Fritz said.

"Not as late as you did in the two-hundred-meters."

It was a cheap and silly riposte, but Fritz did not rise to it. He said simply, "That is true. So I must concentrate on the other race."

His imperturbability, I supposed, was a good quality, but I found it irritating.

Two things happened in the afternoon: Fritz qualified for the finals of the hundred-meters, and Beanpole was eliminated from the high jump. Fritz again came in second, but the winner was yards ahead of him at the tape, and I did not think much of his eventual chances. Beanpole was very depressed by his defeat. Up to the last raising he had been jumping well and confidently, and seemed certain of going through, but at that point his coordination failed him, and in his first jump he went off at half cock and ludicrously hit the bar waist high. His second jump was a good deal better, but still an obvious failure. On the third, I thought he had cleared it but he must have just caught the bar with his foot.

"Bad luck," I said.

His face, as he pulled on the track suit, was white with anger against himself. "How *could* I jump so badly?" he said. "I've cleared a lot higher than that dozens of times. And now, when it matters . . ."

"There's still the long jump."

"I just couldn't get the lift . . ."

"Forget about it. There's no point in brooding."

"It's easy to say that."

"Remember what Fritz said. Concentrate on the other one."

"Yes. I suppose it's good advice."

He did not look convinced.

So we came to the day of the finals. In the evening there would be a procession to the town, where the Feast of the Games was held, with all the competitors honored, especially the victors in their scarlet belts. And the morning after they would parade on the Field, on show for the last time before the Tripods picked them up to take them to their City.

It had been very hot during the night, and the sky was no longer blue but livid with clouds, which looked as though they might open at any moment to pour down torrential rain. Thunder rumbled in the distance. If it did rain, the events were to be postponed to the following day. I stared at the sky from the door of the hut, and prayed that it would hold off. I felt I was tensed to the limit already. I tried to force myself to eat some breakfast, but the food would not go down.

Beanpole's event was scheduled first, mine

second, and Fritz's third. Concentrating on watching him jump was a torment, but at least took my mind off my own prospects. He jumped well, and it was clear that there were only two others who might possibly match him. They were before him in order, and on the first jump there was a matter of inches between their marks, with the rest out of the running. On the second jump their results were much the same, but this time Beanpole outdistanced them to take the lead. I saw him walk back from the pit, brushing sand from his leg, and thought: he has it now.

One of the others fell badly short on the final jump. But the second, a gangling, freckle-faced boy whose hair sprouted in bright ginger tufts through the silver mesh of the Cap, did much better, and his jump put him in the lead. The difference was nine centimeters—about four inches by our English measurement—which was not much in itself but terribly disheartening at this stage. I watched Beanpole tense himself, run down the grassy track, and hurl his body through the humid air. A cry went up. It was clearly the best jump of the day. But the cry turned to a groan of disappointment as the judges' flag was lifted. The jump had been disqualified, and the ginger-headed boy had won.

Beanpole went off by himself. I followed him,

and said, "It couldn't be helped. You did your best."

He looked at me with a blank expression. "I stepped on the board. I haven't done that since the early days of training."

"You were putting too much effort into it. It could happen to anybody."

"Was I?"

"Of course you were."

Beanpole said, "I wanted to win. And also I was frightened about what came next. I thought I was trying."

"We could all see you were."

"In the high jump," he said, "I went to pieces at the crucial moment. And this time I got myself disqualified quite stupidly and unnecessarily. I thought I was trying, but was I?"

"What you're saying is stupid. You were just trying too hard."

The blankness had turned to misery. "Leave me alone, Will," he said. "I don't want to talk at the moment."

The boxing finals were early in the afternoon, and my section provided the second contest. The boy I was fighting was a north German, a fisherman's son. He was smaller even than I was, but compact and well muscled. I had seen him box and knew that he was good, a fast mover and a hard hitter.

For the first minute we circled each other warily. Then he came in at me with a quick left and right, which I parried. I counterattacked, forcing him to the ropes and getting in a right cross to the ribs, which made him grunt as breath was forced from his lungs. But he got away before I could do any further damage. We fought at a distance again, but in the last thirty seconds I carried the fight to him and scored a few times. It was my round, I thought.

I went out confidently for the second. He backed away, and I followed. He was almost on the ropes. I threw a left hook at his jaw. It did not miss by much, but it missed. The next thing I remember was lying on the canvas, with the referee standing over me, counting. ". . . *Drei, vier, fünf . . .*"

It was an uppercut, Beanpole told me later, which did not travel far and caught me under the chin, lifting me and dumping me. All I knew then was that I was at the same time floating in a haze of pain and rooted to the hard boards beneath me. I supposed I ought to get up, but I did not see how I was going to set about it. Nor did there seem much urgency. There appeared to be long intervals between the words that were being chanted, at once close above me and from an echoing distance.

". . . *Sechs, sieben . . .*"

I had lost, of course, but I had done my best,

at any rate. Like Beanpole. I saw his set, bitter face through the haze. "I thought I was trying, but was I?" And what about me? I had been hit because I had dropped my guard. Had something at the back of my mind wanted to do that? Was there even now the beginning of the feeling: you did your best and lost, so no one can blame you? You can go back to the White Mountains, instead of the City of the Tripods. And with it the beginning of a doubt that would not easily be dismissed.

"*Acht!*"

Somehow I got to my feet. I could not see straight, and I was staggering. The boy from the north came after me. I managed to dodge some blows and ride others, but I have little idea how. For the remainder of the round he chased me, and once caught me in a corner and gave me a hammering. I did not go down again, but I knew as I sat on my stool and the cool sponge was rubbed over my flesh that I was desperately far behind on points. I would have to knock him out to win.

He realized this, too. After his first probing had established that I was no longer dazed, he did not try to take the fight to me, but boxed me from a distance. I went after him, but he stood me off. I was gaining a few points, probably, but nothing like the number I had lost.

And the seconds were ticking away on the big wooden clock that stood on the judges' table and was started at the beginning of each round and stopped three minutes later.

In the end I grew desperate. I abandoned my own defense, deliberately this time, and went in hitting as fast and as often as I could. Most of my blows failed to land, whereas he got in a couple to the body that rocked me. But I kept on, fighting not boxing, forcing in the hope that somehow something would give. And it did. He measured me for a punch that would have finished the job the uppercut had started, and missed. And I did not miss with my own hook to the jaw. His knees buckled and he went down, and I was sure he was not going to get up by a count of ten, for that matter, fifty. The only doubt I had was whether the bell would go before the count was completed. I had an idea we were in the final seconds. But my mind had been playing me tricks. I learned, to my astonishment, that less than a minute had elapsed of this last round.

Beanpole and I watched the final of the hundred-meters race in silence, each concealing his different feelings. But our silence was shattered when it became apparent that Fritz was keeping up with the runner who had outclassed him in the previous heat. We were both shouting as the two of them crossed the tape. Beanpole thought Fritz had won; I, that he had just lost. It was some time before the announcement came, and it proved us both wrong. There had been no clear winner. The race would be rerun, with these two competitors only.

And this time Fritz made no mistake. He went into the lead right away and held it to win, if not comfortably, very obviously. I cheered with the others, and fervently. I would far rather it had been Beanpole, but I was glad that, at any rate, I would have one ally when I went into the City.

That evening, during the Feast, the heavens opened, thunder rolled almost continuously, and through the high windows I saw lightning playing across the roofs of the town. We ate wonderful food in enormous quantities, and drank a wine that bubbled in the glass and tingled in one's throat. And I sat at the High Table, wearing my scarlet belt with the rest.

In the morning, as we paraded, a light drizzle was still falling. The Field itself was waterlogged, and our shoes were clogged with mud. I said good-by to Beanpole, and told him that I hoped I would meet him again, and soon, in the White Mountains.

But the hope was a faint and feeble one. The six Tripods stood fixed, as they had been throughout the Games, while the ceremony of farewell was carried out. I looked at the faces of my companions, all happy and exalted at the thought of serving the Tripods, and did my best to put the same expression on my own. My legs trembled. I made an effort and controlled them, but moments later they were trembling again.

There were more than thirty of us, in six groups. I saw the group with Fritz in it go first, marching to the Tripod immediately ahead. The tentacle snaked down as they came close to the great metal foot. It lifted them, in turn, to the hole that opened in the hemisphere, the hole into which, nearly a year before, I had thrown the exploding metal egg of the ancients. I had no defense now, and could have none. I watched the next group go, and the third and fourth. Then it was our turn, and, splashing through puddles, I walked woodenly forward with the rest.

6

---

*The City
of Gold
and Lead*

What chiefly worried me was that my true
feelings would show when the tentacle gripped
me—that I would not be able to avoid straining
against it and marking myself out as different
from the others. I even wondered if the tentacle
could somehow read my thoughts. I remembered the feel of it—hard metal but weirdly re-
silient, pulsing with what seemed like life. When
it was my turn to be lifted, I did my best to
blank out what was happening. I thought in-

stead of my home, of lazy afternoons wandering through the fields, of swimming in the river
with my cousin Jack. Then the breath gasped
from my body as I was plucked up and lifted
through the rain-seeping air. Above me the door
in the hemisphere was open—a mouth growing
larger as I was brought toward it.

I was expecting the lapse into unconscious-
ness, which had occurred in my first encounter
with a Tripod, outside the Château de la Tour
Rouge, but it did not happen. Later I understood
why. The Tripods had a means of doing this,
but they used it only on the un-Capped, who
might panic and struggle. There was no need for
such restraint with those who had learned to
worship them.

The tentacle put me inside and released me,
and I could take in my surroundings. The hemispheres were some fifty feet across the base, but
the part we were in was much smaller, an
irregularly shaped cell about seven feet high.
The outer wall with the door was curved and
had portholes on either side, covered with what
seemed to be very thick glass. The remaining
walls were straight, but the side ones sloped inward, so that the interior wall was shorter than
the external. There was another door there, I
saw, but it was closed.

There were no furnishings of any kind. I ran

my fingernails over the metal and found it hard but satiny in texture. There were six in my group, and I had been the fifth to be taken. The last one was brought in, and the door closed, a raised round flap coming down to make a tight seal. I looked at the faces of my companions. They showed some confusion, but excitement and exaltation as well, which I did my best to copy. No one spoke, which was a help. I would not have known what to say, or how to say it.

Silence for endless minutes, then, abruptly, the floor tilted. The embarkation must have been completed. Our journey to the City had begun.

The motion was extremely odd. The three legs of the Tripod were attached to a circumferential ring beneath the hemispheres. At their points of attachment and where the legs jointed were segments that could lengthen and shorten as the legs shifted relative to each other. There was also an arrangement of springs between the ring and the hemisphere that compensated for much of the jolting. What was left, after the tilt when the Tripod started to march, was a mild rocking movement. It was a little nauseating at first, but one rapidly grew accustomed to it.

The Tripods could travel as easily in one direction as another by reason of their three-legged symmetry, but at present the section we were in represented the front. We crowded to the portholes, and looked out.

Ahead, a little to our right, was the hill with the ancient semicircle of stone steps; behind it, the town where, the night before, we had feasted. Beyond that again was the dark ribbon of the great river. We were going slightly north of east, heading toward it. The countryside beneath us was blurred and wet, but the rain had stopped and there was a patch of brightness in the cloud where the sun might be. Everything was small and far away. The fields and houses and cattle seen in the valley below from the tunnel had been tinier, but that panorama had been fixed, unchanging. Here, change was continual. It was like being in the belly of a huge low-flying bird, flapping its way across the landscape.

Remembering the Tripods whose feet had served as boats, I wondered if these might do so, too, on reaching the river, but they did not. The forward leg sent up a fount of spray as it broke the surface, and the others followed. The Tripod crossed the river bed as a horseman would have forded the stream below my father's mill at Wherton. On the other side, it changed direction, turning south. There was open country, and then desolation.

Beanpole and I had seen something of this brooding ruin of one of the great-cities on our way north. The river had flowed for miles between its black, unpromising shores. But from this high vantage point, one saw so much more. It stretched eastward from the river, a dark and ugly mass of destroyed buildings and broken roads. Trees had grown among them, but to a lesser extent than in the great-city we had crossed on our journey south to the White Mountains. This place seemed to be vaster, and uglier. I saw no remains of broad avenues and concourses, no sense, here, that our ancestors, before the Tripods came, had lived lives of order and beauty. But there was an awareness of might and power, and I wondered again how they could have been defeated—how we, a handful of shattered remnants, could hope to succeed where they had failed.

One of the others saw it first and cried out, and we jostled each other to look. It rose beyond the edge of the ruins, a ring of dull gold standing against the gray of the horizon, surmounted and roofed in by an enormous bubble of green-tinged crystal. The Wall was more than three times as high as the Tripods, smooth and unbroken. The whole place, although resting solidly on the earth, seemed strangely unconnected with it. Some distance from the point for which we were making, a river bubbled up from under the shield of gold, and flowed away toward the mother river behind us. The eye, following its course, could almost imagine that the City was not there at all—that if one looked hard enough the illusion would vanish, and there would be just the river running through ordinary fields. But it did not vanish. The Wall rose higher as we approached, becoming more awful and forbidding.

The sky grew lighter. From one instant to the next, the sun broke through the mask of clouds. Sunlight glistened on the ramparts, reflected from the crystal roof. We saw a great band of gleaming gold, on which flashed a titanic emerald. And I saw a narrow slit of darkness, which widened. A door opened in the seamless Wall. The first of the Tripods marched through.

What happened as our Tripod entered the City was something for which I was completely unprepared. I felt as though I had been struck a savage blow, but a blow that contrived to hit me in every part of my body at the same time, a blow from the front, from behind, most of all from above, smashing me down. I staggered and fell, and saw my companions do the same. The floor of the compartment pulled us as though it

were a magnet and we were flakes of iron. I
struggled to rise, and I realized it was not a
blow, but something different. All my limbs had
turned to lead. It was an effort to raise my arm,
even to twitch a finger. I strained, and stood up.
I was carrying a tremendous burden on my
back. Nor on my back alone—on every square
inch of bone and muscle in my body.

The others followed suit. They looked puzzled and frightened, but they still did not look
unhappy. After all, what the Tripods wished on
them was good; it must be. There was dim green
light. It was as though one were very far down
in a thick forest or in a cave under the sea. I
tried to make sense of it all, but could not. The
weight on my body bowed my shoulders. I
straightened myself up, but felt them sag again.

Time passed, and we waited. There was
silence and heaviness and greenness. I tried to
concentrate on what must be the most important
thing—that we had achieved our first objective
and were inside the Tripods' City. One must
have patience. It was not, as Julius had pointed
out, my most outstanding quality, but I had to
cultivate it now. Waiting would have been easier
without the dimness and the crushing weight. It
would have been a relief to say something, anything, but I dared not. I shifted my feet, seek-
ing a stance of greater ease, but not finding one.

I had been looking at the door on the inner wall, but it was the other that opened, swinging back and up with a faint whirring noise. There was still nothing to be seen outside, just a high dim green. A tentacle came in, and lifted one of my companions out. I realized that it must be able to see, independently of the hemisphere. Might it still be that the Tripods themselves were alive—that we were the captives of living and intelligent machines? The tentacle returned. This time it took me.

It was like a hall, long and narrow but of enormous size, probably eighty feet high and two or three times that in length. I saw that it was a kind of stable for Tripods. Against one wall a long row of them stretched away into the green dusk, faintly illumined by hanging globes that gave a dim green light. Their hemispheres rested close against the wall, far above us. Those in which we had traveled were unloading their human cargo. I saw Fritz, but did not speak to him. We had agreed that no contact should be attempted until the first stage, whatever that proved to be, was safely over. One by one the others joined us. At last the tentacle hung limp and inactive. A voice spoke.

This, too, sounded as though it might have been the voice of a machine. It was deep and toneless, echoing and booming in the vast space.

The words were in the German language that we knew.

"Humans, you have the privilege, the high honor, to have been chosen as servants of the Masters. Go where the blue light shines. In the place to which it leads you, you will find fellow slaves who will instruct you in what you are to do. Follow the blue light."

It had come on while the voice was speaking, a light that glowed deep blue in the base of the wall by which the Tripods were standing. We walked toward it, or staggered, rather, against the drag of this leaden weight that pulled us down. And the air was hotter, I thought, than it had been inside the Tripod, and clammy, like the moment before summer thunder. The light was above an open door, which admitted us to a small room, much the same size as that in the Tripod, but a regular cube. The door closed when we were all in. There was a click and another whirr, and suddenly the weight was even greater, seeming to drag my stomach down with it in a swoop of nausea. This lasted several seconds, and was followed by a brief sensation of lightness. The whirring stopped, the door opened, and we walked out into another room.

This also was large, although modest in comparison with the Hall of the Tripods, but of more conventional proportions. There was the same green glow from lamps that studded the walls. (Their light, I saw, did not flicker the way our lamps did.) I had a confused impression of rows of tables, or benches rather. And of half-naked, old men.

They were the ones who, the voice said, were to instruct us. They wore only shorts, reminding me of men who worked in the harvest fields, but there was no other resemblance. The green light tricked the eyes, but even so I could see that their skins were pallid and unhealthy. But were they as old as they seemed? They walked like old men and their skin fell into the folds of age, but in other ways . . . They came to us, one to each, and I followed my guide to one of the benches. A little pile of articles was laid out there.

Most of them were self-explanatory. There were two pairs of shorts, like the ones our instructors were wearing, two pairs of socks, two pairs of shoes. No, one pair of shoes and one of sandals, the latter, I was told, for indoor wear. But there was also a device that baffled me. He explained it in a tired voice, a south German accent.

"You must put this on before you go through the air lock, and wear it always while you breathe the Masters' air. In the house of your own Master you will have a room, in which to eat and sleep, where you will not need it, but otherwise it must never be removed. The air of the Masters is too powerful for such as we. If you go into it without protection, you will die."

It was like glass in that one could see through it, but was different to the touch. Even the thicker part, which fitted over the head and rested on the shoulders, would yield a little when one pressed it, and it tapered to a thin stuff that molded itself to the body. There was a belt that went round the chest, high under the arms, and could be tightened to hold the helmet on firmly. On either side of the neck were pouches holding a dark green sponge-like material. These had a network of fine holes, on both outside and inside, admitting air. The sponges, it seemed, could filter out the part of the Masters' air that was too strong for their slaves to breathe. My instructor pointed to it.

"This must be changed every day. Your Master will supply you with new ones."

"Who is my Master?" I asked.

It was a foolish question. He stared at me blankly. "Your Master will choose you."

I reminded myself that my policy must be to lie low and say nothing, observing not questioning. But there was one thing I could not avoid asking. "How long have you been in the City?"

"Two years."

"But you're not . . ."

The remnants of pride broke through the heavy dullness of his voice. He said, "I won the thousand-meters race at the Games, less than a month after I was Capped. No one had ever done that before in my province."

I stared at him, at the slumped tired body, the worn, sick-looking flesh, with horror. He was no more than two years older than I was, perhaps less.

"Change into these clothes." His voice was once more blank and expressionless. "Throw your old ones on that pile."

I took off my scarlet champion's belt. "What about this?"

"Put it with the rest," he said. "You do not need it in the City."

We dressed in our new clothes, putting the articles we did not require immediately into a small bag we were given, and fastened on our masks. Then we were marshaled and led away and through a door into another smaller room. The door closed behind us, and I saw there was an identical one on the opposite side. There was a hissing sound and I could feel a breeze over my feet. I realized that air was being drawn into a grille that ran along the base of the wall. But air was also coming in from another grille just above head level. I could feel it, and after a time I thought I could *see* it—thicker, greener in the green light. In some strange way the air was being changed in this room, the ordinary kind being replaced by that which the Masters breathed. It continued for several minutes. Then the hissing stopped, the door in front opened, and we were told to walk out.

It was the heat that struck me first. I had thought it was hot enough inside the Tripod and in the outer rooms of the City, but that was mild in comparison with the furnace blast that I now encountered. And yet not a furnace blast, because the air was damp as well as hot. Sweat started to pour out all over my body, but particularly on my head, encased in its hard, transparent cover. It trickled down my face and neck to the place, high on my chest, where the belt trapped it against my skin. I drew in gulping breaths of hot, stifling air. I felt weak, and the weight dragged me down. My knees started to buckle. One of my companions fell, and then a second and a third. Two of them struggled back to their feet in a moment or two; the third lay still. I thought of helping him, but remembered my resolution not to take a lead in anything. I was glad of the excuse to do nothing. Keeping myself from falling or fainting was difficult enough.

Gradually I became a little more accustomed to things, and could look at what lay in front of us. We had come out on a kind of ledge, and the main thoroughfares of the City lay below us. It was an eye-wrenching confusion. None of the roads was straight, and few of them were level; they dipped and rose and curved between the buildings, and were lost in the dim green distance. The City seemed even vaster inside than it had seemed from the porthole of the Tripod, but I had an idea that was because of the thicker, greener air. One could not really see very far with any clarity. The crystal dome that covered everything was invisible from here; the green dusk seemed to stretch endlessly.

The buildings astonished me, too. They were in different shapes and sizes but of one general form: the pyramid. Immediately below our ledge I saw a number of squat, broad-based pyramids; farther off there were thinner, more tapering constructions that rose to differing heights, the smallest seeming almost as high as the ledge, but others much taller. There were what looked like windows in them, triangular in shape, but dotted about the walls in no kind of pattern that I could understand. It made my eyes tired to look at them.

Strange carriages moved along the ramps. These, too, broadly speaking, were pyramids, but resting on one side rather than on the base. which in this case formed the rear. The top parts were of a transparent material like our helmets, and I could see figures in them, but only very indistinctly. Other figures moved on the spaces between the buildings and the ledges, which jutted from them at irregular intervals. They were of two kinds, one much smaller than the other. Although, at this distance, one could not make out particular features, it was obvious that one kind was the Masters, the other their human slaves, because the smaller creatures moved slowly, as though dragging heavy weights, while the larger ones moved lightly and quickly.

One of our instructors said, "Behold. These are the dwellings of the Masters."

His voice, though muffled, was reverential. (Beneath the pouches with the sponges were small metal devices. These, I found, carried sounds through the mask. The sounds were distorted, but to this, as to other things, one grew accustomed in time.) He raised a pointing hand in the direction of one of the nearer pyramids.

"And there is the Choosing Place. Let us go down."

We made our slow and staggering way down a spiral ramp, whose steepness threw an extra aching strain on the muscles of our legs, causing falls now and then. (The boy who had fainted up on the ledge had revived and was with us. He was the one who had beaten Beanpole in the long jump, the gingery freckle-faced lad who had managed to put that extra effort into his final jump. He would not jump far here.) The heat, too, continued to drain our strength away, and the sweat, running down, formed an unpleasant puddle at the base of the mask. I wanted desperately to wipe it away, but, of course, that was impossible. To do so I would have had to take the mask off and, as I had been warned, this meant death in the air that the Masters breathed.

I still had not seen one of the Masters close enough for them to be anything but a blur. But, at least, one problem was solved. The Tripods were not the Masters, as some had thought, but merely cunningly devised machines that carried them through the world outside. I did not see how this would help Julius and the others much, but it was information. Presumably I would learn more, a lot more. After that, all Fritz and I needed to discover was a way of making our escape. All! I could have laughed at the thought, but lacked the energy. And I had to remember of course, my role, as one of the Capped, a chosen but willing slave.

The ramp led into one of the squat pyramids, about halfway up from the base. Inside there was light from dozens of green globes that hung at varying heights from the ceiling. If anything, the light was brighter than the dusk outside. We were taken along a curving corridor to a long room with a pointed ceiling. Along one side was a row of open-fronted cubicles, their sides made of the hard glass-like substance. Each of us, we were told, was to go into one of these. After that we were to wait. The Masters would come in due course.

We waited a long time. For the others, I imagine, it was easier. Being filled with the desire to serve the Masters, above all things, would give them patience. Fritz and I had no such comfort. He was in a cubicle some ten away from mine, and I could not see him. I could see those on either side of me and, dimly, the two or three after that. I was filled increasingly with tension and apprehension, but knew I must not show it. There was discomfort also. Most of us were sitting or lying on the floor to help relieve the drag on our limbs. Lying was best, except for the sweat that had pooled inside the mask and, uncomfortable anyway, was intolerable if head and shoulders were not upright. By now, also, I was dreadfully thirsty, but there was nothing to drink and no means of drinking, in any case. I wondered if they could have forgotten us—if we were to be left here until we died of thirst and exhaustion. Presumably we were of some value to them, but it would not be much. We could be replaced very easily.

I sensed rather than heard it at first, but it grew into a ripple of sound, spreading along the cubicles to my right—a sound of awe and wonder, maybe of worship. I knew then that the moment had come, and craned my neck to see. They had entered the room from the far end, and were approaching the cubicles. The Masters.

For all the discomfort and fatigue, and my fears as to what might happen, my first impulse was to laugh. They were so grotesque! They stood much taller than a man, nearly twice as tall, and were thick in proportion. Their bodies were wider at the bottom than the top, four or five feet around I thought, but tapered upward to something like a foot in circumference at the head . . . if it *was* the head, for there was no break in the continuity, no sign of a neck. The next thing I noticed was that their bodies were supported not on two legs but three, these being thick but short. Matching them were three arms, or rather tentacles, issuing from a point about halfway up their bodies. And their eyes—I saw that there were three of those, too, set in a flattened triangle, one above and between the other two, a foot or so below the crown. The creatures were green, though I saw that the shades differed, some being dark, the green tinged with brown, and others quite pallid. That, and the fact that their heights varied to some extent appeared to be the only means of telling one from another. I felt it was a poor one.

Later I was to discover that, as one grew accustomed to them, identification was easier than I had expected. The orifices, which were their mouths, noses, and ears, varied too, in size, in shape a little, and in their relationship to each other. They were connected by a pattern of wrinkles and creases that one learned to know and recognize. At first impact, though, they were faceless, almost completely uniform. It sent a shiver of quite a different fear down my spine when one of them, stopping before me, spoke.

"Boy," he said, "stand up."

I thought the words issued from the mouth—which I judged the lower of the two central orifices to be—until I saw that it was the upper one that was quivering and open while the other remained closed and still. With the Masters, I was to discover, the organs of breathing and eating were not connected, as men's are: they spoke as well as breathed through one, and ate and drank through only the lower, larger opening.

I stood up, as I was bid. A tentacle came

toward me, touched me lightly, and then more firmly on the arm. It ran along my flesh, like a snake, with the dry smooth texture of a snake, and I repressed a shudder.

"Move about," he said. The voice was cold, flat, not loud but penetrating. "Walk boy."

I began to walk round the narrow confines of the cubicle. I thought of a horse sale I had seen once at Winchester—men feeling the muscles of the beasts, watching them parade around the ring. We did not need to be paraded; we could parade ourselves. The Master stood in front of me critically while I made several circuits of the cell. Then, with no other word or comment, he moved on. I stopped walking, and let myself slump back into a sitting position.

They traveled fast on those stumpy legs, bouncing off the ground with an up-and-down rhythmic motion. They were clearly vastly stronger than we were to make so light of this leaden City. They could also, when they really wanted to get somewhere fast, spin along like tops, the three legs whirling them round and round and at the same time forward, with yards between each foot touching the ground. I suppose it was their version of running.

The Choosing went on. Another Master came to inspect me, and another. The boy in the next stall was taken; a Master ordered him to follow and he obeyed. They disappeared in the throng. Some Masters examined me more closely than others, but all moved on. I wondered if they were suspicious—if something in my behavior were not quite right. I also wondered what would happen if I were not chosen at all. It was known that no one returned from the City. In that case . . .

This particular worry was unnecessary. Those who were not chosen as personal servants went into a general pool, I discovered. But I did not know that at the time, and was aware of the stalls emptying around me. I saw Fritz go past, following a Master. We looked at each other, but gave no sign. A Master came up to my cubicle, stared at me for a moment, and went on, without speaking.

Their numbers had thinned, as well as ours. I sat on the floor miserably. I was tired and thirsty, my legs were aching, and the skin of my chest and shoulders was beginning to sting from the salt of my sweat. I leaned my back against the transparent wall, and closed my eyes. So I did not see the new Master who came, only heard his voice, commanding me.

"Get up, boy."

I thought it was a pleasanter voice than the others had been, with an undertone in it that might almost be warmth. I struggled to my feet, and looked at him curiously.

Physically, he seemed to be shorter than average, and he was also darker in color. The tinge of brown in the dark green was quite marked. He stared down at me, the skin wrinkling between his eyes, and ordered me to show my paces. I summoned my strength and moved as briskly as I could; perhaps I had been too lethargic for the others.

I was told to stop, and did so. The Master said, "Come nearer."

As I moved toward him a tentacle snaked out and wrapped round my left arm. I gritted my teeth. A second tentacle stroked appraisingly along my body, assessing my legs, reaching up to wind more closely round my chest in a grip that forced breath from my lungs, then withdrawing. The voice said, "You are a strange one, boy."

The words, summing up my chief fears, petrified me. I stared ahead at the featureless column of the monster. There was almost certainly something I should be doing, showing. Excitement? Happiness at the prospect of being allowed to serve one of these absurd and disgusting creatures? I tried to act out that mood. But the Master was speaking again.

"How did you become a champion at the Games—in which of your human sports?"

"Boxing . . ." I hesitated. "Master."

"You are small," he said. "But strong, I think,

for your size. Which part of the land do you come from?"

"From the south, Master. Tirol."

"A mountain land. They are hardy ones, who come from the high parts."

He fell silent then. The tentacle that still held my left arm released it and dropped back. The three eyes stared at me. Then the voice said, "Follow me, boy."

I had found my Master.

7

---

*My Master's
Cat*

I was fortunate in my Master.

He led me to his carriage, which was in a line of others outside the building, showed me into it, and drove us away. The driving would be one of my duties, he explained. (It was not difficult. It was moved by an invisible power that came from below the ground. There was little to do in the way of steering, and collisions were impossible.) I saw that some of the Masters with newly acquired slaves were already forcing them to learn this skill, but mine did not because he saw that I was tired and distressed. The carriage ran on very many small wheels, set beneath one face of a pyramid, and the driver had a seat in the pointed front part for controlling it. My Master drove it to the place where he lived, in toward the center of the City.

On the way I examined my surroundings. It was hard to make sense of the place; buildings and streets and ramps were at the same time very much like each other and confusingly different, their construction either unplanned or following a plan I could not begin to understand. Here and there I saw small areas that I supposed were meant for gardens. They were mostly triangular in shape, and filled with water, out of which grew strange plants of various colors. I saw red, brown, green, blue—but all somber. They all had the same general shape, too: a squatness at the base that tapered with height. Many of the garden pools had mists rising from them, and in some I saw Masters moving slowly about or standing, like trees themselves, rooted in the water.

My own Master lived in a tall pyramid overlooking a large garden pool. It was five-sided but looked more like one of the triangles of which the Masters seemed to be so fond, since three of the sides were shorter than the others and formed almost a straight line. We left the carriage outside the door—I looked back and saw the ground open under it and take it in—and went into the building. At the center we entered a moving room, like the one that had taken us from the Hall of the Tripods. My stomach lurched as it whirred, but this time I understood what was happening—that the room was moving upward and we with it. We came out in a corridor and I trudged along in the Master's wake to the door that was the entrance to his home.

There was much that I understood only later, of course. The pyramid was divided into homes for the Masters. Inside was a smaller pyramid, completely enclosed by the outer one, which was used for store rooms, the place where the carriages were kept, the communal place for slaves, and so on. The homes were in the outer section, and one could tell a Master's importance in the City from the position of his home. Most important was the one right at the top—the pyramid on top of the pyramid. Next came the two triangular homes immediately below, and after that the homes at the corners of the pyramid, in descending order. My Master was only moderately important. His home was on a corner, but nearer the base than the apex.

At first sight of the City, with all its towering

peaks, I had thought the number of Masters must be fantastically great. At closer quarters I realized that the impression had been to some extent misleading. Everything was on a far bigger scale than the human one to which I was accustomed. The homes, in particular, were spacious, the rooms being large and very high, twenty feet or more.

From the corridor one came into a passage with several doors. (The doors were circular, and worked on the same principle as the one in the Tripod: a section swung inward and upward when a thing like a button was touched. There were no locks or bolts.) In one direction, the passage turned through a right angle at the end, and eventually issued into the most important part of the home: the triangular room that looked out from the building. Here the Master ate and relaxed. In the center of the floor was a small, circular garden pool, its surface steaming from extra heat provided beneath it. It was his favorite spot.

But I was not shown this right away. The Master took me along the passage in the opposite direction. It ended in a blank wall, but there was a door on the right a little before that. The Master said, "This is your refuge, boy. There is an airlock inside—that is a place where air is changed—and beyond that you can breathe without the mask. You will sleep and eat there, and you may stay there or in the communal place at times when I do not require your service. You may rest for a while now. In due course, a bell will ring. Then you must fix your mask on again, go back through the airlock, and come to me. You will find me in the window room, which is at the end of the passage."

He turned and glided away, light on his stumpy feet, along the broad high passage. I understood that I had been dismissed, and pressed the button on the door in front of me. It opened and I stepped through, and automatically the door closed behind me. There was a hissing, and I felt the pull of the air current on my ankles as the Masters' air was drawn out and replaced by human air. It did not take long, but it seemed an age before the door on the opposite side opened and I could step through. My fingers were tearing at the fastener of the belt that secured the mask as I did so.

I did not think that I could have supported the stifling confinement, with my own sweat pooling on my chest, for much longer, but later I found that I had been lucky. Fritz had been kept for several hours, being instructed in his duties, before he was allowed to find relief. My Master's consideration was apparent in other ways. The room set aside for the servant was

small in floor area, but had the same towering
height as the rest of the home. In this case the
Master had had an intermediate floor con-
structed, with a ladder leading up to it. My bedroom was up there, whereas in other cases the
bed had to be fitted into the limited living space.

Other than that there was a chair, a table
(both of the simplest kind), a chest with two
drawers, a cupboard for storing food, and a
small toilet section. It was bare, and ugly. There
was none of the extra heat, which the Masters'
rooms had, but no way of cooling, either, or of
freshening. One sweltered, the only alleviation
being in the toilet section, where there was a
device for spraying water on one's body. The
water was lukewarm, both for that and for
drinking, but cooler at least than the surround-
ing air. I let it play over me for a long time,
and washed and changed my clothes. The air
made the clean ones damp before I had put
them on. No clothes were ever dry inside the
City.

In the cupboard I found food, in packets. It
was of two kinds: a sort of biscuit to be eaten
dry and some crumbling stuff to be mixed with
the warm water from the tap. Neither had much
taste, and they never varied. They were made
by machines somewhere in the City. I tried a
little of the biscuit, but I found I was not hungry

enough yet to eat it. Instead I hauled myself
wearily up the ladder, a straining effort in this
City of Lead, and dropped onto the bare, hard
bed that awaited me. There were no windows,
of course, to my quarters, but a globe of green
light in each, turned on and off by a button. I
pressed the button, fell into darkness and oblivion, and dreamed I was back in the White
Mountains, telling Julius that the Tripods were
made of paper, not metal, and that one could
chop their legs off with an ax. But, in the middle
of telling him, there was a savage clangor in my
ears. I awoke with a start, and realized where I
was, and that I was being summoned.

Knowing nothing of conditions in the City,
Fritz and I had not been able to make any
specific plans for finding each other, though
naturally we were anxious to do so as soon as
possible. When I contemplated the size and
complexity of the place, despondency overcame
me; I did not see how we could ever hope to
make contact. There were, plainly, thousands of
Masters in the City, even allowing for the amount
of space each took up. If every one of these had
a servant . . .

In one way it was less difficult than I had
thought; in others, more. To start with, each
Master did not have a servant. It was a privilege

reserved for those of a certain rank, probably less than a thousand in all, and not all availed themselves of the right. There was a movement in opposition to the presence of humans in the City. It was based on a fear, not that the slaves might revolt, because no one doubted their docility, but that the Masters, in accepting the personal service of other creatures, were some- how weakened and degraded. The total number of humans, drawn from the Games and from other selection procedures in other places, was probably no more than five or six hundred.

But between this five or six hundred means of communication were extremely limited. There was, apart from the individual refuges for sleep- ing, eating, and so on, a communal place for slaves in each pyramid where they were kept. In a larger, but still windowless, room it was possible to meet and talk, with a number flash- ing in a box on the wall to tell you when your Master required your return. One could not go to a communal place in other buildings without running the risk of being absent when the call came. And the risk was never taken, not through fear of punishment, but because, to the Capped, it was unthinkable that they should fail the Master in any way.

We might meet on the street or be sent on errands by our Masters, but the odds were against that. It soon seemed obvious that the only real chance of discovering each other lay in both our Masters attending the same function, at which (as was true of most) there was a restroom for slaves.

There were a number of such functions, I discovered. The one of which my Master was fondest was one in which they rooted themselves in a pool inside a pyramid, while in the center a group of them used their tentacles to agitate devices that rippled the water and shook the air and at the same time sent out wild sounds, which my Master found pleasurable but which to me seemed hideous. At another, the Masters spoke to each other in their own language, full of whistling and grunting sounds; in a third, Masters on a raised stage hopped and whirled about in what I supposed was meant to be a dance.

To all these, at different times, I accompanied my Master, and went eagerly to the restroom to shower and dry myself, and perhaps eat a piece of the monotonous biscuit or, at least, lick one of the salt sticks with which we were provided. And to hunt among the other slaves for Fritz. But again and again I drew a blank, and I began to think it was hopeless. I knew that not all the Masters enjoyed these things, just as there were events to which my Master did not choose to go.

It was beginning to seem that we had had the bad luck to be chosen by Masters whose interests were very different.

In fact, this was true. My Master was fondest of things that stemmed from the mind and imagination; Fritz's of those that exercised and demonstrated the body. Fortunately, though, there was one event that had an almost universal appeal. They called it the Sphere Chase.

It took place, at regular intervals, in the Sphere Arena. This was a great open space in the shape, naturally, of a triangle, near the center of the City. It was covered with some reddish substance and there were seven posts, perhaps thirty feet high, each with a basket-like contraption at the top. Three of these were set at the points of the triangle, three midway between the points, and the seventh in the center.

That is as much, really, as I can describe that makes sense. I think that what happened in the arena was a kind of game, but if so it was not like any game that men play. Small Tripods, standing not much more than twenty feet high, issued out from a place below ground behind one point of the triangle, performed a complicated marching about for a time, and then started chasing each other. After a while, in the course of this chase, one or more golden spheres would appear in the air between the probing points of the Tripods' tentacles. This was generally greeted by a full booming noise from the Masters, who were watching from all round in terraced seats. The booming would increase as the chase and pursuit continued with the golden ball flashing and tossing between them. At some stage the sphere would be flung over or around one of the baskets on top of the poles, and eventually would light in the basket, when there would be a great coruscating flash, a noise like a clap of thunder, and the booming from the spectators would be punctuated with wails and howls. This was much intensified when it happened to be the center pole's basket that was hit, both as to flash and thunder and (I imagine) applause. Then the chase began all over again, and a new ball was created.

The small Tripods, I found, were occupied by one or, at the most, two Masters. It seemed that much skill was involved in the Sphere Chase, and those best at it were greatly honored. On that last bit of the trek that Henry and Beanpole and I had made to the White Mountains—when the two Tripods came across us out in the open but took no notice—then, too, there had been the golden ball flashing against the blue sky. I realized that the Masters driving those Tripods must have been Sphere Chasers, practicing for the next Chase and too engrossed to concern themselves with anything else. It represented a weakness in the Masters, trivial, perhaps, but any sign of fallibility was something to rejoice at.

The other good thing was that the Sphere Chase was the means of my finding Fritz, after weeks of fruitless searching. I accompanied my Master to his seat in that side of the triangle reserved for the superior ones, and hurried—which meant a lumbering rather than a dragging walk—down to the restroom beneath. It was larger than any other communal room I had seen, but crowded for all that; there must have been a couple of hundred slaves in it. I pulled off my mask, placed it in one of the lockers along the wall near the entrance, and went looking for him. He was at the far end, in the queue for the salt sticks, which we sucked to replace the salt we lost through our continual sweating. He saw me and nodded, and brought two salt sticks over to where I stood, as far removed from the others as possible.

I was shocked by the sight of him. This was a life, I knew, that would drag anyone down, if only by reason of the relentless clammy heat and the constant drag on bone and muscle. Many of the humans I had met were in a pitiful state, old and enfeebled long before their time. I was conscious in myself that, although I was learning to live with the heat and weight, and to husband my energy, gradually my strength was ebbing. But the change in Fritz was far beyond expectation.

We had all lost weight, but he, who had been tall and well built, seemed, in proportion, to have lost much more than I. His ribs showed painfully through the flesh of his chest, and his face was gaunt. He had the stooped posture that one saw in those who had been a year or more in the City. I saw something else, too, with horror: a pattern of angry marks across his back. I knew that some of the Masters beat their human servants for carelessness or stupidity, using a thing like a fly whisk, which burned the flesh where it touched. But Fritz was not stupid and would not be careless.

Giving me the salt stick, he said, in a low voice, "The most important thing is to make arrangements for future meetings. I am at 71 Pyramid 43. It would be better to meet there, if you have an easy Master."

I said, "Where is that? I still can't find my way about."

"Near the . . . No. Tell me where you are."

"19 Pyramid 15."

"I can find that. Listen. My Master goes to a garden pool almost every day, regularly at two seven. He stays for a period. I think there's time enough to get to your place. If you can manage to get down to your communal place . . ."

"I'll do that, easily."

"I'll be the slave of a visiting Master."

I nodded. We used Masters' time in the City, not human time. The day was divided into nine periods, and each period was divided into ninths. It was made difficult by the fact that the day started with sunrise, and so changed continually. Two seven was approximately noon. My Master, too, often went to a garden pool around then. Even if he did not, I could keep some small errand until that time.

"Your Master," I said, "—is he very bad?"

Fritz shrugged. "Bad enough, I think. I have nothing to compare with."

"Your back . . ."

"He enjoys that."

"Enjoys!"

"Yes. At first I thought it was because I was doing things wrong, but it is not so. He finds reasons. I howl and shriek a lot, which pleases him. I have learned to howl louder, and it does not go on so long. What about your Master? I see that your back is unmarked."

"I think he is a good one."

I told Fritz something of my life, of the small signs of consideration I was given. He listened, and nodded. "A very good one, I would say."

He related a few other things about his own life, from which it was plain that the whippings were far from being the only respect in which he suffered worse than I. In every way possible, his Master humiliated, persecuted, and heaped impossible burdens on him. I was almost ashamed to have been so lucky. He did not dwell on this, though, but said, "Anyway, all that is not important. It is what we find out about the City that matters. We must exchange information with each other, so that what one learns the other knows. You tell me first what you have discovered."

"Very little so far. Practically nothing." I searched my brain for snippets, and retailed them to him. They were a meager collection. "That's all, I think."

Fritz had listened gravely. He said, "It all helps. I have found where the great machine is from which they get heat and light, and the means for making the carriages go. For making the City so heavy as well, probably. Ramp 914 leads off Street 11. It goes through a place with garden pools on either side, and then dips down into the earth. The machine is down there somewhere. I have not been able to go down yet—I am not sure if humans can go there—but I will try further.

"Also, I have found the place where water

comes into the City. It is in Wall Sector 23. A river comes in below ground and passes through another machine that makes the water suitable for the Masters. I have been there, and will go again. It is a huge place and I cannot understand much about it yet. Then there is the Place of Happy Release."

"Of Happy Release?"

I had heard this phrase spoken once or twice by other slaves, but had no clue as to its meaning. Fritz said, "That is not far from here, along Street 4. It is the place where the slaves go when they know they are no longer strong enough to serve the Masters. I followed one, and saw it happen. There is a place where the slave stands, beneath a dome of metal. There is a flashing light, and he drops to the floor, dead. Then the floor on which his body is lying moves. It goes along, and a door opens, and there is a white-hot furnace inside, which burns the body away to nothing."

He went on to tell me what he had discovered about the human slaves in the City. They did not only come from the Games; in other countries they were selected in different ways, but always for youth and strength. The life in the City, even where the Masters, like mine, were tolerant, possibly kind, was one that killed them, slowly but surely. Some crumpled up and died almost at once; others lasted a year, two years. Fritz had met a slave who had been more than five years in the City, but he was exceptional. When the slave knew that death was on him, he went of his own volition to the Place of Happy Release, and died in the glad assurance that he had served the Masters to the utmost of his ability and the last atom of energy.

I listened carefully to all this. Now I was really ashamed. I had been thinking my life was hard, and had been treating this as an excuse for not doing anything much. In effect, I had been marking time, hoping to get in touch with Fritz and then think of what to do. He, with so much worse to suffer, had nevertheless been getting on with the task that we shared, and on which man's future might depend.

I asked him, "How did you manage to find all these things, if you can only get away during the two hours he spends at the garden pool? You could not get to them all in that time, surely."

"There is another Master with whom he has twice spent a day. He is one of those who disapprove of slaves, and my Master leaves me behind. So I got out and explored."

"If he had returned unexpectedly, or called you . . ."

There was a means in each home by which a Master could call his slave to come to him. Fritz said, "I had thought of an excuse. He would beat me, of course, but I am used to it."

There had been an occasion when I had been left behind. I had spent the day resting, talking in the communal center. Once I had gone out, but the confusion of streets and ramps and pyramids had depressed me, and I had come back. I felt myself flushing.

We had been talking apart from the others, but more and more had been arriving from the arena above us, and the room was beginning to be crowded. Fritz said, "Enough now. 19 Pyramid 15. The communal place at about two nine. Good-by, Will."

"Good-by, Fritz."

Watching him lose himself in the throng of slowly moving slaves, I made a resolve: to play my part more keenly, and with less self-pity.

The duties I had to perform for my Master were not in themselves particularly onerous. I had to tidy the home, prepare and serve his food, see to his bath, make his bed—that sort of thing. As far as food was concerned, preparation was easy enough, for it consisted of mixtures of differing texture and color (and flavor, too, I imagine), which came in transparent bubble bags. Some needed to be mixed with water, but many of them were eaten just as they were. Serving was a different matter. Portions of the foods were put on a triangular dish and eaten in a certain order. The placing and the ways in which they were laid out were important. I became good at this quite quickly, and was commended for it. It was a little more difficult than it seems, because there were dozens of patterns that had to be learned.

He had a bath several times a day, in addition to visits to one of the garden pools and wallowings in the smaller pool in the window room: all the Masters soaked themselves in water as often as they could. His private bath was next to the room in which he slept. Steps led up to it, and the bath itself was a hole in which he could put his body to be wholly submerged. The water was specially hot for this; it welled up from the bottom, boiling. I had to put in powders and oils that colored and scented the water, and lay out a number of strange brush-like devices with which he scrubbed himself.

The bed was upright, too, and of much the same shape as the bath, but instead of the approach being by steps, it was up a spiral ramp, a fairly steep one, which it made me pant to climb. Inside was placed a sort of damp moss, and each day I had to remove the old and replace it with fresh from the bed cupboard. Although the moss looked light, it was heavy. I suppose this was the hardest of my tasks, as far as labor was concerned.

But apart from these and other similar duties, there was another function I fulfilled: that of companionship. Except for the occasions on which they joined together to watch the Sphere Chase or other forms of entertainment, the Masters led strangely solitary lives. They visited one another, but not often, and spent a good deal of their time in their homes alone. (Even in the garden pools, I noticed, they did not talk to each other much.) To some, though, this isolation came less easily than to others—to my own Master, I suspected. A human slave to him was not merely something to do various menial chores around the home, not merely a sign that he was of the rank that qualified him to own such a one, but someone who could listen to him talk. In my village at home, old Mrs. Ash had six cats and spent most of her day talking to one or the other of them. I was my Master's cat.

With the advantage of being a cat who could talk back. He not only spoke to me of the things that happened to him (I could rarely make any sense out of them, and I never began to understand what work he did), but he asked questions as well. He was curious about me, and about my life before winning at the Games and coming to the City. At first I was suspicious of his interest, but I quickly realized that it was innocent. So I told him all about the way I had lived as the son of a small dairy farmer in the Tirol, how I had driven the cows up to pasture in the high meadows at the beginning of the day and stayed with them until it was time to bring them back for milking in the evening. I invented brothers and sisters, cousins and uncles and aunts, a whole pattern of life that he accepted and seemed to take an interest in. When I was off-duty, I used to lie on my bed in my refuge and think of more lies to tell him; it was a way of passing the time.

Or it had been until I realized how little I had been doing compared with Fritz. But when I said something about it to Fritz the following day when we met again in the communal place of my pyramid, he took a different view. He said, "You have been very lucky with that one. I had no idea any of the Masters spoke to us slaves, except to give orders. Mine does not, certainly. He beat me again this morning, but he did it in silence. I was the one who made a noise. Perhaps you can learn more from this than from exploring the City."

"If I asked questions, he would certainly be suspicious. The Capped do not pry into the wonders of the Masters."

"Not questions, as such. But perhaps you can

lead him on. You say he talks about his own life, as well as asking you about life outside?"

"Sometimes. But it makes no sense. He has to use their words when he talks about his work because there are no human words for the things he is telling me about. A few days ago he was saying that he was feeling unhappy because during the zootleboot a tsutsutsu went into spiwis, and therefore it was not possible to izdool the shuchutu. At least, it sounded something like that. I saw no point in even trying to understand what it meant."

"If you keep on listening, it may make sense in time."

"I don't see how it can."

"It may, though. You must persevere, Will. Encourage him to talk. Does he use the gas bubbles?"

These were small rubbery spheres that could be stuck to the Master's skin, below the nose opening. When they were pressed by one of the Master's tentacles, a reddish brown mist came out and rose slowly upward, encircling the Master's head.

I said, "He has one a day, sometimes two, when he is in the pool in the window room."

"I think it does to them what strong drink does to men. Mine beats me harder after he has sniffed a gas bubble. Maybe yours will talk more. Take him another while he is in the pool."

I said, "I doubt if it will work."

"Try, anyway."

Fritz looked ill and exhausted. The weals on his back were bleeding slightly. I said, "I'll try tomorrow."

And I did, but the Master waved me away. He asked me how many calves cows bore, and then mentioned that the pooshlu had strool-glooped. I did not seem to be getting very far.

8

The Pyramid of Beauty

When I had just about abandoned hope of getting any useful information out of the Master he solved the problem for me himself. His work, whatever it was, took place in a squat pyramid about half a mile from the one in which he lived. I had to drive him there in the carriage and stay in the communal place with the other slaves until he was ready to return. This would be after two periods (just over five human hours), and I used the time, as the other slaves

did, to rest and, if possible, sleep. One learned
early in one's life in the City the overwhelming
importance of conserving energy to the maximum degree possible. There were couches provided in this communal place. They were hard,
and there were not enough to go round, but it
was a luxury far from being universal, and I
was grateful for it.

On this occasion I had been lucky enough to
get a couch, and was lying on it, drifting into
sleep, when my arm was shaken. I asked hazily
what was the matter, and was told that my number was flashing on the call box, indicating that
I was wanted. My first thought was that it was
a trick to get me off the couch, which the other
slave probably wanted for himself, and I said
as much. But he insisted that it was true. At last
I roused myself to look, and saw that it was.

As I got my mask and prepared to put it on, I
said, "I don't see how the Master can want me.
It's only been three ninths. There must be a
mistake."

The other had taken my place on the couch,
and was lying there prone. He said, "It may be
the Sickness."

"What sickness?"

"It is something that happens with the Masters from time to time. They stay at home for
two or three days, or even longer. It is more

likely with those like your Master, who have brown in their skins."

I remembered that I had thought, that morning, that his skin was darker than usual. When I went to him in the outer room and made the customary deep bow of respect, I noticed that it was very much darker, the brown more pronounced and that his tentacles, even though at rest, were quivering slightly. He told me to drive him home, and I obeyed.

I thought, remembering human sickness, that he might want to go to bed, and realized that I had not yet changed his moss. He did not do that, though, but instead went into the pool in the window room and squatted there, motionless and silent. I asked him if there was anything he needed, and he did not answer. So I went to the bedroom and got on with my work. I had just finished, and was putting the old moss into the cupboard in which it would be destroyed, when the bell rang for me.

He was still in the pool. He said, "Boy, bring me a gas bubble."

I did as I was told, and watched him place it between his mouth and nose and press on it with a tentacle. The reddish brown mist oozed out, almost like a liquid, and rose up. The Master breathed in deeply. This went on, with him taking breaths of it at intervals, until the bubble was empty. He tossed it away for me to pick up, and called for another. This was unusual. He used it and had me bring him a third. He started talking not long afterward.

It did not make sense at first. I gathered he was talking about the Sickness. He spoke of the Curse of the Skloodzi, which seemed to be the name of his family or his race, or perhaps it was the name the Masters gave themselves. There was a lot about wickedness—I was not sure whether he meant his own or that of the Masters in general—but although he bemoaned it, I could not help feeling that he did so with a certain amount of satisfaction. The Sickness was a punishment for wickedness and therefore had to be endured with stoicism. He flicked away the third empty gas bubble with his central tentacle, and told me to get a fourth, and to move faster this time.

The gas bubbles were in the room where the food was kept. I went to bring one, but when I returned to the window room he was out of the pool. He said, his voice even more distorted than usual, "I ordered you to move faster, boy."

Two of the tentacles gripped me and held me in midair as easily as I might hold a kitten. He had not touched me since that first meeting in the Choosing Place, and I was more shocked than anything else. But shock was rapidly re-

placed by pain. The third tentacle whipped
through the air and lashed my back. It was like
being hit by a heavy length of rope. I jerked
against the tentacles that held me, but it did no
good. The lash came down again and again.
Now it felt more like a sapling than a rope that
was striking me. I thought it would break my
ribs, even perhaps my spine. Fritz had said that
he cried out because he realized his Master
wanted him to. I supposed I ought to do the
same, but I would not. I gritted my teeth, crushing a fold of skin between them and sending hot
salty blood flowing inside my mouth. The beating went on. I had given up counting the blows;
there were too many of them. And then there
was a roaring in my ears, and oblivion.

I recovered to find myself lying on the floor. I
moved slightly, and there was pain again. My
body seemed to be one long bruise. I forced myself to get up. As far as I could tell, no bones
were broken. I looked for the Master, and saw
him squatting, silent and motionless, in the pool.

I was humiliated and angry, and aching all
over. I limped from the room and took the passage round to my refuge. Once inside, I stripped
off my mask, dried the sweat from my neck and
shoulders, and hauled myself up the ladder to
my bed. I realized as I did so that I had omitted

the customary bow of reverence to the Master when I left the window room. I had certainly not felt reverential toward him, but that was not the point. The essential thing was in every way to imitate the behavior of the truly Capped. It had been a slip, and could be a dangerous one. As I was thinking of this, the ringing of the bell hammered my nerve endings. My Master wanted me again.

Wearily I descended, put on my mask, and left the refuge. My mind was confused and I did not know what to expect. The thought of another beating was uppermost, and I did not know how I was to endure it; it hurt even to walk. I was entirely unprepared for what did happen when I returned to the window room. The Master was no longer in the pool, but standing near the entrance. A tentacle seized me and lifted me. But instead of the lash for which I was trying to prepare myself, there came, from the second tentacle, a gentle stroking gesture, a snake's soft writhing along my battered ribs. I was a kitten being cuddled after it had been chastised.

The Master said, "You are a strange one, boy."

I said nothing. I was being held awkwardly, with my head slightly lower than my body. The Master went on, "You did not make loud noises as the others have done. There is a difference in you. I saw it that first day in the Choosing Room."

What he said petrified me. I had not realized, though I suppose I should have, that the natural reaction of the Capped to being beaten would be to howl like children. Fritz had sensed this and behaved accordingly, but I had stupidly resisted through pride. And then had failed to make the bow of reverence afterward. I was terrified that the Master's next move would be to probe the Cap with the tip of his tentacle, through the softer part of the mask. If he did, he would soon realize the difference between mine and the true Caps, which knit in with the living flesh. And then . . .

But, instead, he put me down. Belatedly I made the bow of reverence and, because of my soreness and stiffness, nearly overbalanced while doing it. The Master steadied me, and said, "What is friendship, boy?"

"Friendship, Master?"

"There is an archive in the City where those things your people call books are kept. I have studied some of them, being interested in your race. Some of the books are lies, but lies that seem like truth. Friendship is one of the things of which they tell. A closeness between two entities . . . that is a strange business to us Masters. Tell me, boy—in your life before you were chosen to serve, did you have such a thing? A friend?"

I hesitated, and said, "Yes, Master."

"Speak of him."

I talked of my cousin Jack, who had been my closest friend until he was taken to be Capped. I changed the details to the life I was supposed to have led, in the mountainous Tirol, but I described the way we had done things together, and the den we had made outside the village. The Master listened, with apparent attentiveness. He said finally, "There was a link between you and this other human—a link that was voluntary, not forced by circumstances . . . so that you desired to be together, to talk with each other. Is this right?"

"Yes, Master."

"And it happens much with your people?"

"Yes, Master. It is a common thing."

He fell into a silence. It lasted a long time, and in the end I wondered whether he had forgotten about me, as sometimes happened, and whether I should take my leave . . . being careful to remember to bow. But as I was contemplating this, the Master spoke again.

"A dog. That is a small animal that lives with men?"

"Some do, Master. Some are wild."

"It has been stated in one of the books that I

saw, 'His only friend was his dog.' Can this be true, or is it one of the lies?"

"It can be true, Master."

"Yes," he said, "that is what I have thought." His tentacles described a small movement in the air that I had come to recognize as expressing satisfaction. Then one of them wrapped itself, but not roughly, round my waist.

"Boy," said the Master, "you will be my friend."

I was almost too astonished to think. I had got it wrong, I saw. I was not a kitten, after all, in the Master's eyes. I was his puppy!

When I saw Fritz, and was able to tell him of what had happened, I expected him to find it funny, but he did not. He said seriously, "This is a wonderful thing, Will."

"What's wonderful about it?"

"The Masters seemed all alike at first, as I suppose men would to them also. In fact, they differ a great deal. Mine is strange in one way, yours in another. But the strangeness of yours may help us to learn things about them, while with mine"—he forced a grin—"it is merely painful."

"I still dare not ask him things that the Capped would not ask."

"I am not so sure. You should have howled when he thrashed you, but it was because you didn't that he became interested in you. He said you were strange before he told you that you were to be his friend. They are not used to seeing free men, remember, and it would never occur to them that a human could be dangerous. I think you can ask him things, as long as the questions are general, and you keep making the bow of reverence at the right time."

"Perhaps you're right."

"It would be useful to find the archive where the books are. They had the Capped destroy all the books that held the knowledge of the ancients, but I suppose they would not have destroyed them here."

"I will try to find out."

"But go carefully," he warned. He looked at me. "Your task is not an easy one."

He was thinking, I felt, that he could have carried it out a good deal better than I; and I was inclined to agree with him. Where I had stubbornness and pride, he had a watchful endurance. He was looking ill, and had been badly beaten again that morning. The whip his Master used left marks that faded in about forty-eight hours, and these weals were fresh. He had once or twice been beaten with a tentacle, as I had been, and said that, although one ached for longer afterward, the beating itself was not so bad as with the whisk thing. I hated to think of what that must be like.

Fritz went on to tell me of his own latest discoveries. The most useful of these was that he had found a place where there were walls with pictures of stars at night, and the Masters could make these pictures move. In the same pyramid there was a globe, almost as high as he was, turning on a spindle, and the globe was covered with maps. He had not wanted to seem too curious, but there was a part he had recognized as a map of the places we knew: it showed the narrow sea across which Henry and I had come, the White Mountains far to the south, and the great river down which the *Erlkönig* had sailed. And on the map, at a point that he calculated as being roughly our present location, was a golden button, which could only be the City.

As far as he could see, there were two other golden buttons on the globe, both well to the south of this one and situated far apart, one on the edge of a great continent to the east, the other on an isthmus between two continents to the west. They must also represent Cities of the Masters, which meant there were three in all from which the world was ruled. A Master had come into the room at that stage, and Fritz had been forced to move on, acting as though he were on an errand of some kind. But he planned to go back and get the details of the positions more firmly in his head.

I still had nothing that seemed worthwhile to

report. Except that I was to be my Master's puppy. He had said my task was not easy. In one sense, I saw, he was right. But in every other respect his was incomparably the harder. And he was the only one who seemed to be getting anywhere.

My Master's Sickness lasted for several days. He did not go to his place of work and spent a lot of time squatting in the pool in the window room. He breathed the gas bubbles a good deal, but did not beat me again. Occasionally he came out of the pool and picked me up and fondled me, and he also talked to me. Some of it was as incomprehensible as when he had talked about his work, but not all. I found out one day, when the green dusk outside was fading as the sun, behind the dome, slanted out of sight in the west, that he was talking about the Masters' conquest of the earth.

They had come in a vast ship that could move through the emptiness between the worlds and the greater emptiness between the stars that warmed the worlds circling round them. This ship had been propelled at an unimaginable speed, almost as fast, he told me, as a sunbeam travels, but even so the journey had lasted many long years of time. (The Masters, I now realized, lived immensely longer than we did, for this one—and, I think, all the Masters in the City —had made that journey and lived here ever since.) Theirs had been an expedition sent out with the purpose of finding worlds that their people could conquer and colonize, an expedition that had many setbacks and disappointments. Not all stars had planets near them, and where they did these planets were usually unsuitable, for various reasons.

The world from which the Masters came was much larger than the earth, and hotter. Being larger, things on its surface weighed more. The Masters had found some worlds too small and others too big for their purpose, some too cold— being far removed from the central sun—and others too hot. Of the ten worlds circling our sun, ours was the only one that would do, but it had an atmosphere poisonous to them and a gravity too light. All the same, it was thought to be worth conquering.

So the great ship was made to go in a circle round the earth, as the moon does, and the Masters studied the world they were to seize. It seems that the ancients had marvelous machines by which they could speak and show pictures at a distance, and the Masters were able to listen and watch without needing to come close enough for their ship to be seen. They stayed like this for many years, occasionally sending smaller ships in close to examine things that were not shown on the distance-pictures, or not in sufficient detail. Some of the ancients, my Master said, reported seeing these ships, but others did not believe them. This could not have happened with the Masters, but men had this strange thing called lying, in which they told of things that had not occurred, and therefore they did not trust each other.

They recognized that in man they had an enemy who might be formidable. There were all these marvels, like the distance-pictures, the great-cities at the height of their glory and power, and other things, too. Men had already begun to build ships that would take them across the emptiness. They had nothing like the ships of the Masters, but they had started, and they were learning fast. And they had weapons. One of these, I gathered, was of the nature of the iron eggs Beanpole had found in the tunnel below the great-city, but as much more powerful as a bull compared to an ant. With one of these giant eggs, the Master told me, many square miles of land could be scorched and blasted—one of the great-cities itself completely obliterated.

If they had brought their ship down to the earth, and made a bridgehead, that bridgehead would have been destroyed. They had to find a different method. The one they chose lay in a field of knowledge in which they were even more advanced than in star traveling—the understanding and control of the mind.

When, on the journey to the White Mountains, they had put the button under my arm by which the Tripods afterward tracked us, and Henry had said that I must have known it was there, Beanpole had spoken of the man in the circus who could make people go to sleep and then obey his commands. I had once seen such a man with a traveling fair that came to Wherton. This sort of thing, and much much more, was known to the Masters. They could, quite easily, put men to sleep and make them, even without the Caps, obey commands—for a time, at least. But the problem still remained of getting men into a position where their power could be used. It is no good being able to make a rabbit pie unless you can first catch your rabbit.

And they caught their rabbits with the ancients' own marvel: the distance-pictures. These pictures were sent out on invisible rays through the air, and turned back into pictures in millions on millions of homes all over the world. The Masters found a means of suppressing those rays at their source, and sending out in their place rays that made the pictures they wanted. There went with them other rays that made

men's minds receptive. So they watched the pictures, and the pictures told them to go to sleep.
When they had gone to sleep, the pictures gave
them their orders.

This control, as I have said, would wear off
in time, but it lasted for days, and the Masters
made good use of the time. A hundred small
ships landed, and men flocked to them as they
had been told. The Caps were put on their
heads—by Masters at first, but later by men who
had already been Capped. It was a process that
grew as it went on. All that was needed was that
there should be enough Caps, and there were.
The plans had been well laid.

By the time those who had not watched the
pictures realized something of what was happening, it was almost too late to do anything
about it. They were separate, isolated, while the
others were working under the orders of the
Masters, united in one purpose. And by the time
the effect of the commands given by the distance-pictures wore off, enough men had been
Capped to ensure that the Masters would have
only scattered and ineffective opposition to face.
One of the first things the Capped had done was
to take control of the mighty weapons of the ancients. So it was possible for the parent ship to
come down to earth and the first occupation
base to be set up.

That was not quite the end, my Master told

me. Some resistance continued. There were great ships on the sea, and ships that traveled under the sea. Some of these remained free for a time and had weapons with which they could strike from half a world away. The Masters had to track them down to destroy them. One of the undersea ships survived for more than a year, and at the end of that time somehow located the main base. It sent one of the great-eggs through the air, to miss its target only by a narrow margin. In the attack, though, it revealed its own position, so that the Masters could use a similar weapon of their own, and sink it.

On land there was sporadic fighting for years, though diminishing all the time because the number of the Capped grew while the number of the free diminished. The Tripods stalked the earth, guiding and helping their followers against bands of men whose weapons were puny, or nonexistent. In the end, there was peace.

I said, "So now all men are happy, having the Masters to rule and help them, and there are no more wars and wickedness." It was an expected comment, and I tried to put as much enthusiasm as possible into it.

The Master said, "Not quite all. Last year a Tripod was attacked and the Masters in it killed when the poisonous air broke in on them."

his dog liked to have. Is there anything you wish, boy?"

I hesitated a moment, and said, "I like seeing the wonders of the City, Master. I would be happy to see more of them."

"That may be done." The tentacle, with a final pat, withdrew, and he began rising out of the pool. "Now I desire to eat. Prepare my table."

The following day the Sickness had abated, and the Master returned to his work. He gave me a thing to wear on my wrist, and explained that anywhere in the City this would make a sound like many bees when he wanted me. I was to come to him then, but otherwise I could wander about: it was not necessary, for instance, that I stay in the communal room of the work place.

I was surprised that he had remembered my request and had done this, but more was to follow. He actually took me out on sightseeing expeditions. Some of what I saw was uninteresting, and some incomprehensible. There was one small pyramid with nothing in it but colored bubbles that moved in a slow dance up to the apex and down the sloping sides. What the Master said about it made no sense to me at all. And there were several trips to water gardens, larger versions of the garden pools, which meant a lot of standing and sitting about while he waded through the seething waters. He invited me to admire their beauty, and I dutifully did so. They were quite hideous.

But he also took me to the place Fritz had spoken of, with the turning globe that had maps all over it, and the walls of bright stars that moved against deep blackness when the Master spoke words, in his own tongue, into a machine. These were star maps, and in one of them he showed me the star from one of whose planets the Masters had set out, long long ago. I tried as well as I could to memorize its position, though it was hard to see what good that would do.

And one day he took me to the Pyramid of Beauty.

A thing that had puzzled me since first coming into the City was that all the slaves were boys. Eloise, the daughter of the Comte de la Tour Rouge, had been chosen Queen of the Tournament and afterward had gladly gone, as she told me, to serve the Tripods in their City. I had thought I might meet her here; it was something I wanted and did not want at the same time. It would have been terrible to see her worn down like all the other slaves, her beauty crushed under the weight and clammy heat of this place. But I found no girls, and Fritz, when I asked him, said he had seen nothing of them either. But on this afternoon, dragging myself along beside my Master, the sweat pooling beneath my chin, I saw them.

It was not one pyramid, but a series of pyramids that joined together near their bases—half a dozen smaller peaks clustered about a central one. It lay a long way, two ninths (more than half an hour, that is) from the part in which my Master lived, by carriage. I saw many Masters strolling about, a few with attendant slaves. We went into the first pyramid, and I almost cried out at what lay before me: a garden of earthly flowers, with that brightness of reds and blues, yellows and pinks and whites that I had almost forgotten, surrounded by a perpetual green twilight, and seeing only the drab, ugly plants of the garden pools.

I realized that I could not touch them: they were protected by the glass-like material from the atmosphere of the City. But it took me longer to realize something else: that despite the appearance of life, there was only death here. I saw this first when I noticed, on the crimson velvet of a rose, the golden bead of a bee. It did not move. Looking further, I saw other bees, butterflies, all kinds of pretty insects, but all still. And the flowers themselves were stiff and lifeless.

It was a pageant, a show by which the Masters could see the real life of the world they had conquered. There was even white light, not green, inside, which made the colors shine with a dazzling intensity. Further on was a forest glade, with squirrels on the branches, birds somehow suspended in space, a rippling stream, and on its bank an otter with a fish between its jaws. But all frozen, dead. It was nothing like the world I had known, once the shock of false recognition had worn off, because the world I had known had been a living, moving, pulsating one.

There were dozens of different tableaus, some of them unfamiliar to me. One showed a dark dripping swamp, not unlike some of the Masters' garden pools, with a couple of strange creatures floating in it that might have been queerly shaped logs but for their gaping jaws, gleaming with vicious white teeth. Some were being rearranged by Masters with face masks somewhat similar to the ones we slaves wore, and my Master told me that they were all changed in turn. But they were only exchanging one dead scene for another.

The Master had a special objective in view, however. We passed all these on our way to the central pyramid. There, a ramp moved up in a narrowing spiral, with egress to different floors. I toiled up after him. I was, as always, tired after a quarter of an hour's walking, and the ramp was quite steep. We did not go out at the first egress. At the second, he led me through a triangular opening, and said, "Look, boy."

I looked, and the salt sweat on my face was mixed with the saltier flow of tears—tears not just of grief, but of anger, more anger, I think, than I had ever felt before.

The vicar at Wherton had a room he called his study, and in it had a cabinet of polished wood, with many thin drawers. I was sent to him once, on an errand, and he pulled the drawers out and showed me what they held. Under glass there were rows and rows of butterflies, pinned down, their gay wings outstretched. I thought of that as I stared at what was exhibited here. For there were rows of caskets, all transparent, and in each casket lay a girl, dressed in her finery.

The Master said, "These are the female humans who are brought to the City. Your people choose them for their beauty, and they are winnowed out again by those Masters who make this place. There are discards from time to time, but the really beautiful ones will be preserved here forever, to be admired by the Masters. Long after the Plan."

I was too full of hate and bitterness to pay attention to the cryptic remark about the Plan. If only I had one of those iron eggs we had found in the great-city . . .

He repeated, "To be admired by the Masters forever. Is it not a fine thing, boy?"

Choking, I said, "Yes, Master. A fine thing."

"It is some time since I looked at them," the Master said. "This way, boy. There are some fine specimens in this row. At times I doubt the destiny of our race, to spread far out across the galaxy and rule it. But at least we appreciate beauty. We preserve the best of the worlds that we find and colonize."

I said, "Yes, Master."

I have said that I both wanted and did not want to find Eloise in the City. Now, in this hideous place, the wanting and the not wanting were increased a thousandfold. My eyes searched hungrily for something from which they could only turn away, in sickness and revulsion.

"Here they all have red hair," the Master said. "Uncommon in your race. The shades of red are different. Observe that they are arranged from light red to deep. I see that there are two new intermediate shades here since my last visit."

It was not red hair my eyes sought, but black —dark hair that I had seen once only, a fuzz growing through the silvery mesh of the Cap, when I had playfully snatched her turban from her in the little garden between the castle and the river.

"Do you wish to go on, boy, or have you seen enough?"

"I would like to go on, Master."

The Master made a small humming noise, which was a sign that he was pleased. I suppose he was glad to think he was making his slave-friend happy. He led the way, and I followed, and at last I saw her.

She was dressed in the simple dark-blue gown, trimmed with white lace, that she had worn at the tournament, when the forest of swords flashed silver in the sun, and all the knights acclaimed her as Queen. Her brown eyes were closed, but the ivory of her small oval face was delicately flushed with rose. But for the casket, very much like a coffin, and the hundreds of others around her, I could have thought she was sleeping.

But her head was bare of both crown and turban. Her hair had grown in the weeks that followed that time in the garden. I looked at her close-cropped curls. They covered, but did not quite conceal, the one thing she did wear on her head: the Cap that had brought her, gladly, to this monstrous resting place.

"Also a fine specimen," said the Master. "Have you seen enough yet, boy?"

"Yes, Master," I told him. "I have seen enough."

9

I Strike
a Desperate
Blow

The days and the weeks went by. There was always the green dusk, but sometimes the twilight was less dim, and then one knew that outside it was a fine summer day, the sun scorching in a high blue heaven. What one saw inside the City was a pale disk, only visible when it was near the zenith, a small circle of lighter green. But the heat did not vary, nor the crushing weight of one's body. And day by day the heaviness and the hotness drained strength away. Each night I lay down with greater thankfulness on my hard bed; each morning it was more of an effort to rise.

Matters were not helped by the fact that the Master became more and more obviously attached to me. His fondling of me, occasional at first, became a daily ritual, and I was pressed into doing something of the sort in return. There was a place on his back, above the rear tentacle, that he liked to have rubbed and scratched. He would urge me to do this more vigorously, and direct me to spots a little higher or lower. I wore my fingernails down against his tough abrasive hide, and he still called for more. Finally I found an implement—a thing vaguely like a brush but curiously shaped—that produced the same, or a similar effect. This saved my fingernails, but not the muscles of my right arm, as he continued to prod me to further exertion.

One afternoon while doing this I slipped and, his body turning round at the same time, the implement brushed lightly against the other side of him, between his nose and mouth. The result was startling. He gave forth a wild howling noise, and a moment later I was flat on my back, smashed to the ground by a reflex action of two of his tentacles. I lay there half stunned. The tentacles reached for me again, and I was sure that now I was in for another beating. But he lifted me to my feet instead.

strains, were not yet so worn out that they needed to go to the Place of Happy Release. A slave had been put in charge of it, and had eventually been allowed to choose an assistant, who became his successor. It had carried on since then, unsupervised and for the most part disregarded by the Masters. When a slave collapsed he was taken to the hospital if he did not quickly recover on his own account. He stayed there, resting, until either he was better or decided that his Happy Release was due.

There was no need for supervision, of course, since the thing the slaves most desired was to serve their Masters or, if they were no longer capable of serving, to end their lives. I found Fritz in a bed a little way off from the others who were patients at the time, and asked him what had happened. He had been sent on an errand after a beating, with no chance to freshen up in his refuge, and had collapsed on the way. I asked him how he was now, and he said better. He did not look much better. He said, "I am going back to the Master tomorrow. If he has taken another slave, then I go to the Choosing Place to see if another Master wants me. But I do not think any will. There is a new batch due shortly, from Games they hold in the east. They will not want one as feeble as I am."

I said, "Then you will go into the general pool? It may be better."

"No." He shook his head. "Only the new ones who are unclaimed do that."

"Then . . ."

"The Place of Happy Release."

I said, horrified, "They can't make you do that!"

"It would seem strange if I did not want to do it, and we must do nothing that seems strange." He managed a poor sort of smile. "I don't think it will happen. The new ones have not yet arrived, so my Master will wait also. He will take me back for a while at least, I think. But I must not stay here longer than is necessary."

I said, "We must do more about finding a way out of the City. Then, if something like that did happen to one of us, he could escape."

Fritz nodded. "I have thought of that. But it is not easy."

"If we could get into the Hall of the Tripods, and steal one. We might be able to find out how to work the mechanism that drives it."

"I do not think there would be much chance. They are twice as tall as we, remember, and all the things they use in the City—except those like the carriages, which are designed for us to work—are out of our reach. And I do not see

how we could get into the Hall of the Tripods.
We would have to go through the Entering
Place, and we would have no excuse for being
there."

"There must be some way of escaping."

Fritz said, "Yes. We have learned many things
that Julius would like to know. One of us must
get back to the White Mountains."

On my way back from the hospital, and later,
I thought about Fritz. If his Master had taken
another slave, after all, and refused to have him
back. . . . Even if not, he was so weak, and
growing weaker. It was not just the beatings:
his Master deliberately gave him tasks that were
beyond his strength. I tried to remember the
time, not so long before, when I had resented
him for usurping, as it seemed, Henry's place on
our expedition. Now, although we saw each
other only at intervals and for brief periods, I
felt closer to him than I had ever felt to Henry
or Beanpole—as though we were brothers.

One enjoys friendship most when times are
good, when the sun shines and the world is kind.
But it is the sharing of adversity that knits men
together. We were both slaves of these monsters,
and, of all the slaves in the City, only we two
understood what was being done to us: that they
were monsters we were forced to serve, not gods
whom it was a joy to wait on. The misery of

this was a bond uniting us. I lay awake a long time that night, worrying about him and trying to plan some way of escape from the City. It was he, plainly, who would need this first. All sorts of crazy notions flitted through my head—such as scaling the inside of the golden wall and cutting a hole through the glass-like stuff that formed the dome. I lay and sweated and despaired.

The next day I saw Fritz again. He had left the hospital and his Master had taken him back. He had beaten him again already. The urgency of discovering a way out had retreated, but not far.

I had wondered at one time why the Masters had taken the trouble to learn our languages rather than make the slaves learn theirs, but it was obvious really. The Masters lived far, far longer than normal men, and the slaves in the City were mayflies by comparison. A slave would be worn out by the time he could understand enough to be useful. There were other factors, too, I imagine. By this means, the Masters retained a privacy of expression among themselves. It was also true that they had a way of learning which men did not: they did not need books but somehow passed knowledge from mind to mind, and so it was easier for them to acquire skills of this kind. My Master spoke German to me, but he could speak to other slaves from other lands in their language. This amused him: the division of men into different races that could not understand each other. The Masters had always been of one race, it seemed, solitary in themselves yet part of a unity that men, even before the Masters came, had shown small signs of achieving.

Like other human things, apart from amusing it also in a way attracted him. He had studied mankind more closely than most of the other Masters had—he read the old books, and he still plied me with questions—and his attitude toward us was a strange one. It combined contempt and disgust, fascination and regret. This last came to the fore when he was in one of his melancholy moods—minor phases of the Sickness—and stayed for long periods in the garden pool, inhaling gas bubbles. It was during one of these phases that he told me something more about the Plan.

I had taken him a third gas bubble, and been forced to submit to the usual caressing from tentacles slimy from the pool, when he started bemoaning the fact that this wonderful friendship we had could only last so short a time, since I, his dog, destined anyway for a brief human life, must have it curtailed still further by the conditions under which I lived in the City. (It did not occur to him that the curtailing might be prevented by having me released to a normal life outside, and I could not, of course, suggest it without letting it appear that I preferred such a thing to a year or two of glorious misery as his slave.) This was not a new topic. He had dwelt on it before, and I had done my best to look puzzled and adoring and ineffably contented with my lot.

On this occasion, though, the professed unhappiness about my approaching death turned into a form of speculation, and even doubt. It began on a personal level. He had asked me again about my life before I came to the City, and I painted for him the picture, a combination of truth and falsehood, that I had outlined before. (I am sure that sometimes there were inconsistencies, but he did not appear to notice them.) I talked of children's games we had played, and then of the Christmas Feast, which I knew was roughly the same in the south as it had been at Wherton, except that, in the mountains, there was more likelihood of snow. I told him of the exchanging of gifts, the service in the church and the feast after—the roast turkey stuffed with chestnuts and surrounded by glistening brown sausages and golden potatoes, the flaming plum pudding. I described it with some poignancy, because my mouth, despite the heat and my growing weakness, watered at the thought, contrasted with the dreadful food that kept us alive here.

The Master said, "One cannot share another creature's pleasure, even a lower creature's, but I can tell that this was a joy to you. And if you had not won at the Games, you would have gone on having such joys through many years. Do you ever think of this, boy?"

I said, "But by winning at the Games, I was permitted to come to the City, where I can be with you, Master, and serve you."

He was silent. The brownish mist had finished rising from the gas bubble and, without being bidden, I rose and brought him another. He accepted it, still silent, put it in place, and pressed it. As the mist rose he said, "So many of you, year after year—it is a sad thing, boy. But nothing compared with the night feeling that comes when I think of the Plan. And yet it has to be. This is the purpose of things, after all."

He paused, and I remained quiet and eventually he began to talk again. He talked about the Plan.

There were, as I have said, several differences between the world from which the Masters came and the earth. Their world was bigger, so that objects on it weighed much more, and also were hotter and wetter. These were things that did not greatly matter. In the City were machines that made the heaviness that I knew only too well, but the Masters could have lived without them. The present heaviness was less than had existed on the home planet, and they or their successors could learn to live naturally on a world like this. As for the heat, there were parts of the earth, it seemed, that were hot enough—in the far south where the other two Cities were.

But there was, of course, another difference to which they could not adapt themselves: the fact that our atmosphere was as poisonous to them as theirs to us. This meant that outside the enclaves of the Cities they could go only masked, and not just head-masked as we slaves went here, but with their whole bodies covered by a clinging greenish envelope, because the brightness of the sun's light hurt their skins also. In fact, except on extremely rare occasions, they never left the shelter of the Tripods—in this cold part of the earth, never at all.

All this, though, could be changed, and would be. The success of the expedition, the conquest of this world, had been reported back to the home planet. Samples had been taken of air, water, and other natural constituents. Their wise men had studied them, and in due course the message had been sent: the earth's atmosphere could be altered to enable the Masters to live naturally in it. The colonization would in due course be a complete one.

It would take time. Mighty engines had to be created, and while some parts of them could be made here, others had to be shipped across the gulfs of space. Once they were set up, at a thousand different places on the earth, they would take in our air and breathe out an air suited to the Masters. It would be thick and green, like the air inside the City's dome, and as it spread the sun's light would dim and the living things that now flourished—flowers and trees, animals and birds and men—would choke and die. Within ten years of the setting up of the engines, it was calculated, the planet would be fit for the Masters' habitation. Long before that the human race would have perished.

I was appalled by what I was told, by the revelation that man's subjugation was not, as we had thought, a final evil, but the precursor of annihilation. I managed to make some inane remark, to the usual effect that whatever the Masters desired was good.

My Master said, "You do not understand, boy. But there are some of us who are saddened by the thought that the things and creatures now living on this world must be blotted out. It is a heavy burden to the mind."

I pricked my ears up. Was it possible that the

Masters were divided among themselves, for all that they professed not to understand man's divisions? Was there a possibility of disunity, and could we exploit it?

He continued, "Those of us who feel like this believe that places should be made where some of the creatures could go on living. The Cities, for instance. Things could be arranged so that some men and animals and plants were able to shelter in them. And the Masters could visit them, masked or in sealed carriages, and view these creatures—not dead as they are in the Pyramid of Beauty, but alive. Would this not be a good thing, boy?"

I thought how much I loathed him, loathed all of them, but smiled, and said, "Yes, Master."

"There are some who say this is unnecessary, a waste of resources, but I think they are wrong. After all, we appreciate beauty, we Masters. We preserve the best of the worlds we colonize."

Places where a handful of men and animals could live, under glass, to satisfy the curiosity and vanity of the Masters . . . "We appreciate beauty . . ." There was a silence, in which we thought our different thoughts. It continued, but the need to know the answer to the vital question pressed in on me. I had to take the risk of asking him. I said, "When, Master?"

A tentacle moved, in a gesture of interrogation. "When . . . ?" he repeated.

"When will the Plan start, Master?"

He did not reply for a moment, and I thought he might be surprised by my query—suspicious, even. I could read some of his more obvious reactions by this time, but there was a great deal hidden. He said, "The great ship is well advanced on its journey back to us, with the things that are needed. In four years, it will be here."

Four short years before the engines began to belch out poison. Julius, I knew, had been assuming that we had time enough—that the next generation, or the one after that might carry the campaign we had started to a final success. Suddenly time was an enemy, as implacable as the Masters themselves. If we failed and an attempt had to be made next year, we should have lost a quarter of the cruelly short interval in which it was possible to act.

The Master said, "It is a splendid sight when the great ship glides through the night like a shooting star. I hope you will see it, boy."

He meant that he hoped I would live that long; four years represented a very good span of life for a slave in the City. I said fervently, "I hope so, Master. It will be a glorious and happy moment."

"Yes, boy."

"Can I bring another gas bubble, Master?"

"No, boy. I think I will eat. You may prepare my table."

Fritz said, "Then one of us *must* get away."

I nodded. We were in the communal place at Fritz's pyramid. There were half a dozen other slaves present, two of them playing a game of cards, the remainder lying flat and not even talking. It would be the beginning of autumn in the world outside; the air this morning would have a nip in it, perhaps, after an early night frost. In the City the sweltering heat did not change. We sat apart, and talked in low voices.

I said, "You haven't found anything, I suppose?"

"Only that the Hall of the Tripods is impossible. The slaves who work in the Entering Place have nothing to do with those inside the City. They are ones who were not chosen by Masters, and they envy those whom they pass through into the City. They would not let anyone through in the opposite direction."

"If we could trick our way in—attack them . . ."

"There are too many of them, I think. And there is another thing."

"What?"

"Your Master told you about the Tripod being destroyed. They know there is some danger, but they think it is only from un-Capped boys. If they find out we have managed to get into the City, wearing false Caps . . . they ought not to have that warning."

"But if one of us escapes," I argued, "won't that be enough to warn them, anyway? None of the truly Capped would want to leave the City."

"Except through the place of Happy Release. There are no checks on who goes there. It must seem as though that is what has happened, and therefore the escape must be secret."

"Any kind of escape is better than none. We have to get this news to Julius and the rest."

Fritz nodded, and I was conscious again of his thinness, his head, although gaunt, large against the frail stalk of his neck. It must be he who escaped, if only one could do so. With a Master kind by their standards, I could hold out for a year or more. He had said he hoped I would see the great ship returning in its glory. But Fritz would not live through this winter unless he got away: that was certain.

Fritz said, "I have thought of one thing."

"What is it?"

He hesitated, and said, "Yes, it is better that you should know, even if it is only an idea. The river."

"The river?"

"It comes into the City, and is purified and

made right for the Masters. But it flows out, also. Do you remember that we saw, from the Tripods, the outflow beyond the walls? If we could find the place inside the City . . . there might be a possibility."

"Of course." I thought about it. "It will probably be on the opposite side of the City from where the river flows in."

"Probably, though it need not be. But that is the part where the Masters who do not have slaves live. One cannot search there as easily, for fear of drawing attention to oneself."

"It is worth trying. Anything is worth trying."

Fritz said, "As soon as we find a way out, one must go."

I nodded. There was no doubt of that, nor of whom the one should be. I thought of the loneliness of staying behind, with no friend in this hideous place, no one to talk to. Except, of course, my Master. That only added a further shudder to the prospect. I thought of the autumn world outside, the early snows already falling and lying on the White Mountains, covering the entrance to the tunnel for another half a year. I looked at the clock on the wall, marked in periods and ninths—Masters' time. In a few minutes I would have to put on my mask and return to take my Master home from his work.

It happened four days later.

I had been sent on an errand by the Master. One of their habits was to rub various oils and ointments into their bodies, and he told me to go to a certain place and get a particular oil. It was something like a shop, with a narrowing spiral ramp in the center and items laid out at different heights. I say a shop though no one was in charge, as far as I could see, and it seemed that no money was paid. This pyramid to which I was sent was much farther away than the ones I customarily went to. I presumed the oil he wanted—he gave me an empty container to identify it—was not available nearer at hand. I slogged my way across the City, taking well over an hour to get there and back, and returned exhausted and soaked with sweat. I wanted desperately to go to my refuge—to take off the mask and wash and rub myself—but it was unthinkable that a slave should do that without first reporting to his Master. So I went the other way, to the window room, expecting to find him in the pool. He was not there, but in a far corner of the room. I went to him, and made the bow of reverence.

I said, "Do you wish the oil now, Master, or shall I put it with the others?"

He did not answer. I waited a moment or two,

and prepared to go away. It might be one of his times of being withdrawn and uncommunicative. Having done my duty, I could put the oil in the cupboard and go to my refuge until he called me. But as I turned one of his tentacles snaked out, caught and lifted me. More fondling, I thought, but it was not that. The tentacle held me up, the unwinking eyes surveyed me.

"I knew you were a strange one," said the Master. "But I did not know how strange."

I made no reply. I was uncomfortable but, having grown used to the license he granted me and, to some extent, to the strangeness of his moods, not apprehensive.

He went on, "I wished to help you, boy, because you are my friend. I thought it might be possible to make more comfort for you in your refuge. In one of the story books of your people, it tells of a man making for a friend what is called a surprise. This I wished to do. So I sent you away, and put on a mask and went in to the refuge. I discovered a curious thing."

It had been held behind him by another tentacle, and now he produced it and showed it to me: the book in which I had written the notes of what I had learned. I was anxious now, all right. Desperately I racked my mind to think of something to say, some explanation, but nothing came.

"A strange one," he repeated. "One who listens, and writes down in a book. For what purpose? The human who wears a Cap knows that the things concerning the Masters are wonders and mysteries, which it is not good for men to learn. I have talked of them, and you have listened. You were my friend, were you not? Though even so it was odd that you showed little fear of being told that which was forbidden. A strange one, as I said. But to record afterward, in secret, in your refuge . . . The Cap should forbid that absolutely. Let us examine your Cap, boy."

Now he did what I had feared might happen on the day he beat me, the day he called me back and told me I was to be his friend. While a tentacle held me in midair, a second one moved to the lower part of the mask, where the material was soft, and its hard tip probed upward. I wondered if it would break through the material, so that I would choke in the poisonous air, but it did not. I felt the tip, narrowing to needle point but hard and precise, run over the edge of the false Cap I was wearing. It probed and plucked.

"Strange, indeed," said the Master. "The Cap is not married to the flesh. Something is wrong here, very wrong. It will be necessary to investigate. You must be examined, boy, by the . . ."

The word he said meant nothing: I suppose he was talking about a special group of Masters who had to do with the Cappings. What was clear was that my situation was desperate. I did not know whether they could read my mind under examination or not, but at least they would know of the existence of the false Caps, and be alerted against our enterprise. They would obviously check all other slaves in the City. In which case, Fritz, too, was lost.

It would be useless to fight against him. Even fully fit, with normal weight, a man was no match for the strength of the Masters. The tentacle had me round the waist, so that my arms were free. But what was the good of that? Unless . . . The central eye, above the creature's nose and mouth, stared at me. He knew something was wrong, but he still did not think of me as a danger. He did not remember what he had told me once when I was rubbing him and my arm slipped.

I said, "Master, I can show you. Bring me closer."

The tentacle moved me in toward him. I was no more than two feet away. I canted my head to the right, as though to show something concerned with the Cap. That movement hid the start of my next one, until it was too late for him to parry or push me away. Bunching my muscles,

I put every ounce of strength I possessed into an upward-swinging right hook. It caught him where the implement had brushed him, between nose and mouth, but this time with the full force of my body behind it.

He gave a single howl, which broke off in mid-cry, and at the same time the tentacle holding me hurled me away from him. I hit the floor hard, some yards away, and slid to the very edge of the garden pool. I was barely conscious as I staggered to my feet, and almost fell into the steaming waters.

But the Master had keeled over as he threw me. He lay there, prone and silent.

10

---

*Under
the Golden
Wall*

I stood by the pool for a moment, trying to
think of what to do. I was dazed from being
dashed to the ground, and dazed also by what
I had achieved. With much the same blow that
had despatched my opponent in the final at the
Games, I had knocked out one of the Masters.
Now that I had done it, it seemed incredible. I
stared at the great fallen figure, with wildly con-
flicting feelings. Astonishment and pride were
mixed with fear; even without being Capped,

it was impossible not to feel awe for the power
these creatures had, for their size and strength.
How had I, a mere human, dared to strike at
such a one, even in self-defense?

These feelings faded, though, in a more acute
and practical apprehension. What I had done
had been unpremeditated, forced on me by the
predicament in which I found myself. My situation now was only to a degree less urgent. By
striking a Master I had irretrievably shown my
hand. I had to decide what action to take next,
and decide quickly. He was unconscious, but
for how long? And when he recovered . . .

My instinct was to flee, to put myself as far
from this place as possible, as quickly as possible. But to do that, I realized, was merely to
exchange a small trap for a larger one. I could
be tracked down so easily in a place where I
could not long survive without going into a
refuge or a communal place—where the other
slaves, once alerted, would be watching for the
fiend who had dared raise a hand against the
demigods.

I looked across the room. All was still, except
for the sparks rising, one by one, in the small
transparent pyramid by which the Masters measured time. He had not moved. I remembered
again what he had said: a Master could be hurt
by being struck in that spot. A Master might

even be killed. Was it possible? Surely not. But he had not moved; his tentacles stretched out limp against the floor.

I had to know the truth, which meant examining him. There were places, as with men, where veins ran close to the surface, where, despite the abrasive toughness of their skin, one could feel the slow heavy beat of their blood. I must check for that. But at the thought of approaching him, fear came back, redoubled. Once again I wanted to run for it, to get out of the pyramid while the going was good. My legs were trembling. For a moment, I could not move at all. Then I forced myself forward, reluctantly, to where my Master lay.

The tip of one of the tentacles lay nearest to me. I reached down, fearfully, touched it with a shudder, drew back, and then, making a great effort, lifted it. It was slack and fell limply when I dropped it again. I went closer, knelt by the body, and felt for the vein than ran to the base of the tentacle, between it and the central eye. There was nothing. I pressed again and again, overcoming my repulsion. No throb at all.

I stood up and away from him. The incredible was more incredible still. I had killed one of the Masters.

Fritz said, "Are you quite sure of it?"

I nodded. "Positive."

"When they sleep, they look as though they're dead."

"But the pulse still beats. I've noticed it, when he fell asleep once in the garden pool. He's dead, all right."

We were in the communal place at Fritz's pyramid. I had sneaked into his Master's home, attracted his attention without the Master seeing me, and whispered urgently that we must meet and talk. He had come down a ninth later. He had guessed something important had happened, because neither of us had approached the other in this way before. But the truth stunned him, as it had earlier stunned me. Following my assurance that the Master really was dead, he was silent.

I said, "I'll have to try to get out somehow. I thought I would try for the Hall of the Tripods, even though the chances are against it. But I thought I'd better tell you first."

"Yes." He braced himself. "The Hall of the Tripods is no good. The best chance is the river."

"But we don't know where the outflow is."

"We can look for it. But we shall need time. When is he likely to be missed?"

"Not until his next duty."

"When is that?"

"Tomorrow. Second period."

It was late afternoon. Fritz said, "That gives us the night. It is the best time for searching, anyway, in a place where slaves are not expected to be. But there is something that must be done first."

"What?"

"They must not discover that someone wearing a Cap is capable of defying the Masters, of striking and killing one."

"It's a bit late, now that I've done it. I don't see how we could get rid of the body, and even if we did, he's going to be missed."

"It might be possible to make it seem an accident."

"Do you think so?"

"We must try. He told you that being struck in that place might kill, so it has probably happened in the past, though not through being attacked. I think we must go there at once and see what we can do. There is an errand I have been saving up, which will be my excuse. But better not together. You go, and I will follow in a few minutes."

I nodded. "All right."

I hurried back across the City, but found my steps faltering as I reached the familiar pyramid and stood outside in the corridor for several seconds, trying to make up my mind to press the button that opened the door. Perhaps I had been wrong. Perhaps there had been a faint pulse that I had not detected, and by now he had recovered. Or perhaps he had been found by another of the Masters. It was true their lives were solitary, but they did sometimes visit each other. It could have happened, by ill luck, today. The impulse to run away was strong. I think it was only the realization that Fritz was coming after me that nerved me to the point of going in.

Nothing had changed. He lay there, motionless, silent, dead. I stared at him, once more bemused by the awareness that it had really happened. I was still staring when I heard Fritz's footsteps approaching.

He, too, was awed by the sight, but recovered quickly. He said, "I think I have a plan. You told me he used the gas bubbles?"

"Yes."

"I have noticed that my Master is confused when he has taken many—in his movements as well as his mind. Once he slipped and fell in the garden pool. If it could seem that this had happened with your . . ."

I said, "He's a long way from the pool."

"We must drag him over there."

I said doubtfully, "Can we? He'll be a tremendous weight."

"We can try."

We dragged him by his tentacles. The touch

was hateful, but I forgot that in the effort to move him. At first he seemed rooted to the floor, and I thought we should have to abandon the idea. But Fritz, these days so much weaker than I, was straining his gaunt body against the load, and it shamed me into pulling harder. He moved a little, then more. Slowly, panting and sweating even more profusely than usual, we dragged him, with many rests, across the room to the pool.

We had to get into the pool ourselves to complete the job. It was very hot, only just bearable, and an unpleasant ooze squelched beneath our feet at the bottom. The water came up to the belt that secured our masks. We waded out, brushing our way through rubber-like plants, some of which clung to us. We really had to heave now on the tentacles, concerting our pulls and moving the body over the side in sharp jerks. Then suddenly the point of balance was reached, and it half toppled, half slid after us, rolling into the water like a heavy log.

Climbing out, we stared down at him. The Master floated on the steaming water, three quarters submerged, one eye staring sightlessly upward. He took up almost the full width of the pool.

I felt too exhausted to think. I could have dropped to the floor and lain there. But Fritz said, "The gas bubbles."

We opened half a dozen, pressed them to release the brown mirk, and scattered them about
the edge of the pool, as the Master would have
thrown them after use. Fritz even thought of
climbing back into the pool and attaching one
of the bubbles to the Master. Then together we
went to the refuge, stripped off our masks,
washed, and dried ourselves. I needed a rest,
and urged Fritz to do the same, but he said he
must get back. It was more important than ever
to take no unnecessary chances. Night was almost on us; the green lamps would be lighting
up outside. He would return now. When I was
ready, I must follow, and wait for him in the
communal place at his pyramid. He would come
down when his Master was in bed, and together
we would go in search of the river.

When he had gone I lay down for a while, but
I was afraid of falling asleep—of waking to find
another Master here and the death discovered.
So I roused myself and made preparations. I
tore out those pages of the book on which I had
scrawled notes, placed them in an empty container, and disposed of the rest of the book in
the cupboard that destroyed waste. I stoppered
the container and put it inside the mask before
I strapped it on.

A thought struck me, and I took two more
small containers and left the refuge. I filled one
with water from the pool, allowed the other to

fill with the Masters' air, and sealed them both. Then I returned to the refuge and put these. too, inside the mask where they rested against my collarbone. Julius and the others might find them useful.

That was, of course, providing we got out of the City. I tried not to think of the odds against it.

I had to wait a long time for Fritz, and when he did come I saw that his back and arms were newly marked with weals. He said yes, he had been beaten for being late on the errand. He looked tired and ill. I suggested that he stay behind and rest while I searched for the river on my own, but he would not hear of it. I was hopeless at finding my way in the City and would only wander around in circles. This was quite true: I had only slowly learned to trace a path through the maze, and then just to certain familiar spots.

He said, "Have you eaten lately, Will?"

I shook my head. "I wasn't hungry."

"But you must eat, all the same. I have brought food down. Drink as much as possible, too, and take a salt stick. Change the sponges in your mask before we go out. We do not know how long it will be before we can breathe good air again."

This was true also, and I had thought of none

of it. We were alone in the communal place. I swallowed the food he gave me, crumbled a salt stick and ate it, and drank water until I thought I was likely to burst. Then I changed the sponges in the mask and strapped it on. I said, "I suppose there's no point in wasting time."

"No." His voice was muffled by his own mask. "We had better start right away."

Outside it was dark, except where the lamps cast small circles of green luminescence; I thought they looked like gigantic glowworms. The heat had not abated, of course. It never did. Almost at once sweat began to form inside my mask. We walked on, with the rolling, lurching gait that slaves developed as the best way of coping with the heaviness in their limbs. It was a long way to the sector where Fritz thought the river might make its exit. One of the carriages would have taken us there quite quickly, but it was unthinkable for slaves to travel in a carriage unless a Master were with them. We had to make it on our own plodding feet.

There were few Masters about, and we saw no slaves. On Fritz's suggestion we split up, with him traveling ahead of me, just within range of visibility. One slave out at night could be explained as being on an errand for a still active Master; two together would seem odd. I saw the point in this, though I regretted the isolation, and was hard put to keep him in sight while staying the distance apart he had suggested. We moved from one pool of light to the next and there was a stage between them where one walked through near blackness, with the next lamp no more than a dim green glow, ahead. It was a strain on eye and mind alike, particularly in the follow-my-leader role that I had to adopt.

One could detect the approach of a Master some way off. Their three round splayed feet made a distinctive flat slapping sound on the smooth hardness of the road. Now I heard this behind me as I passed under a lamp. It grew louder, since they moved faster than we did. I thought it might come abreast of me in the dark patch, and wanted to dodge away. But there was no side turning here, and, anyway, it might look suspicious. There was the possibility of losing touch with Fritz, as well. I walked on, remembering a few lines of poetry I had found in an old book at home:

> Like one, that on a lonesome road
> Doth walk in fear and dread,
> And having once turned round walks on,
> And turns no more his head;
> Because he knows a fearful fiend
> Doth close behind him tread.

I had not turned round, but then I did not need to, knowing very well what it was that followed. We were in a part of the City entirely strange to me, and I suddenly realized that if I were questioned I had no sort of answer to give. I tried to think of one, but my brain had gone blank.

The dark patch came, and the sounds were still behind me. He should have been up with me by now, I thought. I had a dreadful conviction that he had slowed his progress deliberately, that he was examining me and would accost me. I went on, expecting every moment that the Master's voice would boom out from behind, a tentacle, possibly, grasp me and swing me off the ground. I could see Fritz's figure dimly, fading into the darkness past the next light. The light itself was approaching. I wanted to strain my muscles into a lumbering run, but somehow kept to my resolution. The slapping footsteps were right behind me, much louder, it seemed, than I had ever heard them before. And then past, and I felt like collapsing in the weakness of relief.

But more was to come. Fritz had already vanished into the next patch of darkness, and the Master disappeared in turn. I made my way after them. Light faded, leaving nothing but the distant glow. This brightened again. I could see the globe of the lamp, lifted on its long angular arm. And just beyond it . . .

The Master was there, and so was Fritz. They stood together, the Master's tall shape towering over Fritz. I heard the distant sound of speech.

I wanted to stop, to turn back into the shadows, but that might attract his attention. I had to go forward, whatever happened. And retreat would mean abandoning Fritz. I marched on. If he were in trouble . . . I did not think much of my chances of landing another punch like the one that had killed my own Master. I found myself trembling, with fear and resolution. Then, with a second surge of relief, I saw the Master move on and Fritz, more slowly, follow.

He waited for me in the next shadows. I said, "What was it? What did he want to know?"

Fritz shook his head. "Nothing. He thought he recognized me as the slave of someone he knew. I think he had a message to give. But I was not the one he wanted, so he went on."

I drew a deep breath into the mask. "I thought we were sunk."

"So did I."

I could not see him in the darkness, but I could hear a tremor in his voice. I said, "Do you want to rest?"

"No. We'll go on."

An hour later we did rest. There was an open place with a large triangular garden pool, to one side of which trees something like weeping willows, only on a massive scale, drooped their branches down to the ground beside the pool, screening us, once we were inside their shelter, from the view of anyone who passed. Though in fact we had seen no one on the streets or ramps for some time now, and there was no sign of a Master in or near the pool. We stretched out under the ropy fronds that, although there was no wind or breeze in the City, from time to time brushed lightly against us. The ground pulled us down still, but it was bliss not to fight it, to lie flat and motionless. I would have liked to clear the inside of my mask of sweat, but even that discomfort was no more than a minor irritant.

I said, "Have you been in this part of the City before, Fritz?"

"Once only. We are not far from the edge."

"And opposite where the river comes in?"

"Roughly opposite."

"So when we find the Wall, we can start looking for the outflow."

"Yes. We shall have to be more careful from now on, of course. It is late to be on a night errand, and we are reaching the part where the Masters who have no slaves live. We must go more warily."

"They don't seem to travel about at night, either."

"No. That's lucky. But we can't be absolutely sure of it. Do you feel thirsty?"

"A bit. Not much."

"I do. It does no good to think about it, though. Since there are no slaves in this part of the City, there will be no communal places." He rose slowly to his feet. "I think we had better get on, Will."

We saw strange things in our search. One of these was a vast pit, a triangle a hundred yards along each side, where, far down, green light gleamed on a seething viscous liquid in which, at intervals, bubbles slowly rose and popped. In another place there was a complicated structure of metal rods and catwalks looming up into the dark night, pointing, it seemed, to lights that flashed high above our heads. Once, turning a corner ahead of me, Fritz stopped, but beckoned me to come up with him. I did so quietly, and together we stared at the scene. It was a small garden pool, with only a few low-lying plants. In it were two Masters, the first we had seen since coming into this sector. They were locked together in what looked like deadly combat, tentacles interlaced, heaving against each other, the water turbulent with their struggling and rolling. We watched for a moment or two and then, making nothing of it, turned silently and went another way.

In due course we reached the Wall. We came down a ramp between two small pyramids, and it was there. It stretched away on either side, golden even in the dim green light of the lamps, curving inward slightly as it was lost in the distance. The surface was smooth and hard and unbroken, offering not even a toe-hold, and upward as well as to the sides it showed no change as far as the eye could see. It was discouraging to look at it.

I said, "Do you think we are near where the river ought to be?"

I saw Fritz's thin ribs rise and fall in the lamp light. I was exhausted, but he much more so. He said, "We should be. But the river would be below ground."

"Will there be a way of getting down to it?"

"We must hope there is."

I looked at the featureless Wall. "Which way do we go?"

"It doesn't matter. Left. Do you hear anything?"

"What?"

"The sound of water."

I listened intently. "No."

"Nor do I." He shook his head, as though to rouse himself. "Left will do."

Thirst began to attack me soon after. I tried to dismiss the thought, but it came back insistently. We were searching for water, after all. I thought of it, cold, crystal clear, like the streams that ran down below the White Mountains. The picture was a torment, but I could not put it out of my head.

We investigated wherever there was a ramp leading down. We found ourselves in weird labyrinths, some piled high with crates, drums, metal spheres, and others packed with machinery that whined and hummed and sometimes sparked. Most of it was untended, but in one or two places there were two or three Masters doing things at boards covered with little holes and pimples. We were treading warily and softly, and they did not see us. In one great cavern gas bubbles were being made. They rolled out of the jaws of a machine down a sloping V-shaped channel and dropped into boxes, which, as they were full, closed themselves and were automatically moved away. In another place, even bigger, food was being manufactured. I recognized it, by the color and shape of the bubble bag, as being a kind of which my Master was especially fond. Had been fond, I corrected myself. The thought gave me a twinge of panic. Had the body been found yet? Were they already looking for his missing slave?

Going back up a ramp to the surface, Fritz said, "I think left was wrong, perhaps. We have come a long way. We must turn back, and try in the other direction."

"Rest first."

"For a few minutes." He sounded discouraged. "We have not much time."

So we plodded back along the way we had come, stopping every now and then to listen for the rushing sound of distant water, but hearing only the noise of the machines. We reached the point at which we had come to the Wall, and toiled on. I became aware of a difference, and looking up, saw the blackness of the night tinged behind us with faint green. The night was coming to an end. Dawn was breaking, and we were no nearer to finding a way out, no nearer to the elusive river.

The day brightened. Thirst overrode hunger, but physical weakness seemed greater than either. The green globes winked out. We saw a Master in the distance, out in the street, and hid behind the edge of a garden pool until he had gone. A quarter of an hour later, we had to dodge two more. I said, "The streets may be swarming with them soon. We will have to give it up for tonight, Fritz, and get back to a place where we can take our masks off and eat and drink."

"In a few hours they will find him."

"I know. But what else can we do?"

He shook his head, "I must rest."

He lay down, and I lowered myself to lie beside him. I felt giddy with weakness, and thirst tore at my throat like a furious animal. Fritz seemed to be in a worse case still. At any rate, we could not stay here. I told him we ought to get up, but he did not answer. I got to my knees and pulled his arm. Then he said, his voice suddenly kindled with excitement, "I think . . listen."

I listened, and heard nothing. I told him so. He said, "Lie down and put your ear to the ground. Sound travels better that way. Listen!"

I did and, after a moment, heard it: a thin rushing sound that might be the whisper of distant tumultuous waters. I pressed my ear closer to the surface of the road, hurting my face against the hardness of the mask. It was there, all right, a torrent underground. Thirst was sharpened even more by the tantalizing sound ot it, but I felt I could ignore that, too. At last we had found the river. That is to say, we knew approximately where it was. The actual finding might take quite a bit longer.

We tried systematically all the downward ramps in the area, testing them by listening to the ground. Sometimes the noise was louder, sometimes fainter. Once we lost it altogether, and had to cast back on our trail. There were avenues that were deceptively promising but that led to dead ends. More and more often we had to dodge Masters, or lie low till they had passed. One promising ramp led to a huge hall in which a score or more of them did things in front of benches: the river might well be somewhere at the far end, but we dared not go through. And time was passing; above ground we were in full day. Then, quite unexpectedly, we came on it.

A very steep ramp, on which we found ourselves slipping and in danger of falling, led across a level space and dipped again, curving round on itself. Fritz clutched my arm and pointed. Ahead lay a cavern with a pointed roof, in which there were stacks of crates the height of a man. At the far end, only dimly visible in the light of the green globes that hung at intervals from the ceiling, water gushed from a huge hole and formed a pool, some fifty feet across.

"Do you see?" Fritz asked. "The Wall."

It was true. At the end of the cavern, beyond the pool, was the dull gleam of gold, unmistakably the inner surface of the barrier that ringed the City, and on which the great dome rested. The pool frothed against it. The water gushing in was that which had circulated through the City, the waste and overflow of hundreds of garden pools. Steam rose up from it. It filled the pool, and from the pool . . . It must go out, under the Wall: there could be no other explanation.

Cautiously we made our way along the cavern, between the stacked crates, to the edge of the pool. There were things like vertical nets in the water, and we saw also that the water steamed only at its entry point. Nearer to the Wall, Fritz reached down and put a hand in it.

"It is quite cool here. The nets must take the heat out, so it is not lost to the City." He stared down into the churning depths, green from the lamps hanging over them. "Will, let the current take you. Before you go, I will put sealer on the air vents of your mask. There is enough air inside a mask to give you five minutes' breathing. I have tried this out."

What he called "sealer" was a substance the Masters used for closing containers that had been opened. It came out of a tube liquid, but dried and hardened almost right away.

I said, "I'll do yours first."

"But I am not coming."

I stared at him. "Don't be silly. You must."

"No. They must not suspect anything."

"But they'll do that when they find I've gone."

"I do not think so. Your Master died from a fall, an accident. What would a slave do, then? I think he might go to the Place of Happy Release, because there is no point in him going on living."

I saw the force of the argument, but said dubiously, "They might think that, but we can't be sure."

"We can help them to think it. I know some of the slaves in your pyramid. If I tell one that I saw you, and you said that was where you were going . . ."

I saw that, too. Fritz had worked things out very well. I said, "If you escaped, and I went back . . ."

He said patiently, "It would not help, would it? It is your Master that is dead, not mine—you who should go to the Place of Happy Release. If you go back, they will question you. It would be fatal."

"I don't like it," I said.

"It doesn't matter what you like, or I like. One of us must get away to take the news of what we have learned back to Julius and the others. It is safer if it is you." He squeezed my arm. "I will get out. It is easy now that I know where the river is. In three days, I will tell the other slaves in my pyramid that I am too sick to work, and therefore have chosen the Happy Release. I will hide out of the way, and come down here at night."

I said, "I will wait for you outside."

"Wait three days, no longer. You must get back to the White Mountains before winter sets in. And now you must hurry." He forced a smile. "The sooner you dive, the sooner I can get back, and have a drink of water."

He spread the sealer on the air vents of my mask, after first telling me to take a deep breath. In a few seconds he nodded, indicating the seal was hard. He pressed my arm again and said, "Good luck." The sound was fainter, more muffled than usual.

I dared delay no longer. The surface of the pool was about six feet below the top of the low containing wall. I climbed up on this and dived down, deep down, into the swirling waters.

11

Two Go Home

Down, down, into darkness. The current tugged me, and I went with it, pulling myself through the water in a crude and feeble attempt at swimming. I swam forward as well as down. My hand touched something and, as my shoulder banged painfully against it, I knew I was at the Wall. But still unbroken, with no sign of an opening, and the current still dragging down.

Possibilities and fears crowded in on me. The water might flow out through gratings, which

I would be unable to remove. Or there might be more nets, and I would tangle myself in them. The whole enterprise seemed hopeless. There was a pressure of air in my lungs, the beginning of a roaring in my head. I breathed out a little, and drew a small breath of air in. Five minutes, Fritz had said. How long had I been under already? I realized that I had no idea; it might be ten seconds, or ten times that. Panic, the fear of drowning, clutched me, and I wanted to turn and swim back up, against the pull of water, up to the surface where I had left Fritz.

I swam on and down, trying to blank my mind to everything but the need to hold on. If I abandoned things now we were lost, anyway. And we must not lose. One of us had to get through. Far above me there was a dim green radiance, but darkness was all round and below me, and I was diving deeper into it. I took another shallow breath, to ease my aching lungs. I wondered if I were already past the point of no return. Then there was turbulence, the current breaking up and changing direction. I reached forward, but there was still an impassible solidity. Down, down . . . An edge, an opening. The tide carried me into it and I realized that now, finally, I was committed. The current was stronger, more closely channelled. I had to go on because there was no hope of getting back.

So I swam and was carried along, in utter blackness. I took shallow breaths when I felt I must. Time, as it passed, became more and more immeasurable. There was a sense of having been hours down here, not minutes. Occasionally I bumped my head against the hard surface above me; if I swam down a few feet I could touch the bottom of the conduit. Once my outstretched hand brushed against a side wall, but I was too concerned with getting through to want to establish how wide it might be.

The shallow breaths were no longer enough: I had to breathe more deeply. And this did not help, either. I was breathing in my own exhaled breath. I felt a hammering inside my head. A blackness was growing there, to match the blackness of the water. It was all hopeless, a trap with no way out. I was finished, and so was Fritz, and those we had left behind in the White Mountains—all mankind. I might as well give up, stop struggling. And yet . . .

It was the faintest of glimmers at first, something that only inextinguishable optimism could read as light. But I flailed on with my weary arms, and it grew. Brightness filtering through —white light, not green. It must be the end of the tunnel. The pain in my chest was savage, but I found I could almost ignore it. Nearer, brighter, but still out of reach. Another stroke, I told my-self, and another, and another. The brightness was right over me, and I kicked and fought my way up to it. Brighter and brighter, and a burst-ing through to the eye-piercing brilliance of the earthly sky.

The sky, but not the air for which my tor-tured lungs were crying out. The sealed mask held me. I tried to release the buckle of the belt, but my fingers were too feeble. I was be-ing carried downriver, the mask buoying me up. Buoying, and also suffocating. I tried again, and failed again. What a terrible irony, I thought, that I should have come so far, only to choke to death in freedom. I clawed at the mask, in-effectually. I was filled with a sense of failure and shame, and then the blackness, for so long barely held at bay, swooped down and swal-lowed me.

My name was being spoken, but from a long way off.

"Will . . ."

There was something wrong about that, I thought drowsily. It was my name, but . . . pronounced in the English fashion, not with the initial "V" to which I had grown accustomed since we had been speaking German. Was I dead, I wondered? In Heaven, perhaps?

"Are you all right, Will?"

Did they speak English in Heaven? But it was English with an accent—a voice I remembered. Beanpole! Was Beanpole in Heaven, too?

I opened my eyes, and saw him kneeling above me, on the river's muddy bank. He said, with relief, "You *are* all right."

"Yes." I gathered my scattered senses. A bright autumn morning—the river flowing beside us— the sun, from which my eyes still automatically turned away—and, farther off . . . the great rampart of gold, topped by the vast green crystal bubble. I really was outside the City. I stared at him.

"But how did you get here?"

The explanation was simple. When Fritz and I had gone, taken by the Tripods, he had intended to go back to the White Mountains and tell Julius what had happened. But he had not been eager for it, and had stayed in the town a few days, listening for anything that was said that might be useful. One thing he learned was the approximate site of the City, and he thought he might as well go and take a look at it. It lay, he was told, across a tributary of the great river down which we had come together. He took the hermit's boat and paddled south and east.

Having found it, he decided to survey it. He dared not risk approaching the Wall by day, but on nights when there was moonlight—some, but not too much—he made his investigations. The result was not encouraging. There was no break in the Wall, and no hope of scaling it. One night he dug down several feet, but the Wall continued still farther, and he had to fill in the hole and leave as dawn broke. None of the Capped approached the City, so he was safe from their attentions. There were farms within reach, and he lived on what food he could pick up or steal.

Once he had been right round the City, there seemed little point in staying on. But it was then that the thought occurred to him, too, that if anyone were going to escape, the river provided what was probably the only feasible route. Its waters, plainly, were waste from the City: nothing grew on the banks for a mile downstream; there were no fish, though there were plenty in the part of the river above the City; and he found strange items of debris from time to time. He showed me some—various empty containers, including a couple of empty gas bubbles, which ought to have gone into one of the waste cupboards but had found their way into the river instead. One afternoon he saw something quite large floating in midstream. It was too far for him to see clearly, particularly since his eyes,

without his lenses, were weak, but he took the
boat out and salvaged it. It was of metal, hollow
so that it floated, measuring some six feet by
two, and a foot thick. If that could come out
of the City, he argued, a man could. In fact it
was hard to see any other way in which an escape was possible. Because of that, he resolved
to take up a position where he could watch the
outflow—watch, and wait.

And so he had stayed here, while the days
and the weeks went by. As time passed, his hopes
that one of us might get away dwindled. He
had no notion of what things were like inside
the City: we might have been discovered on the
first day as falsely Capped, and killed. He stayed
on, more, he said, because leaving would mean
abandoning the last shred of hope than because
hope had anything to feed on. Now, with the
autumn, he realized that he could not delay
much longer if he were to get back to the White
Mountains before the heavy snows. He had decided to give it another week, and on the morning of the fifth day had seen something else
floating downriver. He had taken the boat out
again, found me, and with a knife had ripped
open the soft part of the mask, to let me breathe.

He said, "And Fritz?"

I told him, briefly. He was silent, and then
said, "What do you think the chances are?"

I said, "Not good, I'm afraid. Even if he finds

his way back to the river, he's much weaker than I am."

"He said he would try in three days?"

"Yes, three days."

"We'll keep a close watch. And your eyes are better than mine."

We gave him three days, and three times three days, and three days beyond that, each time finding a less convincing argument for our vigil. Nothing came out of the City, that we could see, but ordinary debris. On the twelfth day there was a snowstorm, and we huddled, shivering, cold, and hungry, under the upturned boat. The next morning, without discussion, we set out under a watery sun peering through gray clouds, toward the great river and the south.

Once I looked back. The snow was melting, but the land still stretched bare and white on either side of the river. The river was a gray arrow in the alabaster desert, pointing to the circle of gold and the dome of green crystal. I lifted my arm. It was still a positive joy to be free of the leaden weight that had crushed me for so long. Then I thought of Fritz, and the joy turned to sadness, and a deep and bitter hatred against the Masters.

We were going home, but only to arm ourselves and others. We would come back.